Dear Diary:

Alex and I are on the road to being a couple. After all these years, my dreams are finally coming true. It didn't take much for him to notice me. All I needed was a little work...new hairstyle, straight teeth, better clothing. Except now, it's not only about being with him that I'm dreaming about. I can actually see **our** future when I look in **his** eyes. I can picture the children we'll have, how they'll look, what color hair and eyes they'll have. Because no matter how we feel about each other, the most important thing is how our children feel about us and the life I know we can give them...together.

ΛΛΛΛΛΛΛΛΛΛΛΛΛΛΛ

❧ FAMILY ❧

ΛΛΛΛΛΛΛΛΛΛΛ

∽FAMILY∽

Emilie
RICHARDS

Good Time Man

Published by Silhouette Books
America's Publisher of Contemporary Romance

SILHOUETTE BOOKS
300 East 42nd St.,
New York, N. Y. 10017

ISBN 0-373-82181-6

GOOD TIME MAN

Copyright © 1986 by Emilie McGee

This edition published by arrangement with Harlequin Books S.A.

® and TM are trademarks of Harlequin Books S.A., used under license.
Trademarks indicated with ® are registered in the United States Patent
and Trademark Office, the Canadian Trade Marks Office and in other
countries.

Visit us at www.romance.net

Printed in U.S.A.

Dear Reader,

Families come in all sizes and constellations. They always have and always will, although these days we're more willing to talk about different ways of creating them.

My own family consists of a daughter by adoption and three sons born to us, and the adoption experience is one of the most memorable of my life. I will always be grateful to *my* Jessie's birth parents, who brought her into this world and made the best decision they could when it became clear they couldn't raise her themselves. I have wished a thousand times that I could tell them so.

This book was written for all parents who have been forced to make difficult decisions and all children who have benefited from their love.

Happy reading,

Emilie Richards

Please address questions and book requests to:
Silhouette Reader Service
U.S.: 3010 Walden Ave., P.O. Box 1325, Buffalo, NY 14269
Canadian: P.O. Box 609, Fort Erie, Ont. L2A 5X3

Prologue

The man loosened the knot of his tie and then seemed to think better of it. Instead, he slipped the longest piece of bronze silk through the knot and folded the tie into uneven squares to stuff it in his pants pocket. The simple act had taken only thirty seconds, but at least for that half a minute it had been something to do. The rest of his wait didn't promise to be as interesting.

"Hurry up!" A reedy male voice echoed down a nearby stairwell and was quickly followed by the clomp of cleats on the wooden steps.

"I'm ready! You're the one who's going to make me late!" a girl's voice answered.

As the man watched, a gold-and-black blur streaked past the living room door, followed by another blur of blue denim.

"Molly? Clancy?" An attractive woman with a harried expression was the next to pass. She thrust her head out the front door and yelled at the retreating blurs. "Get in the car. We'll leave in a minute." Then she turned and smiled nervously at the man. "How do I look?"

"Beautiful." He stood and gave her a warm grin.

"Are you sure you want to do it like this, Alex?" The woman's face was contorted into a worried frown. "Are you sure you don't want me to stay and wait with you?"

"We discussed it at length, remember? This seems like the easiest way. I'll wait for Jessie here, and then I'll bring her to the restaurant to meet all of you. It'll be more casual that way."

"I don't feel casual!"

Alex moved to her side for a reassuring hug. "Lydia, I'm sure I can't really understand how you feel right now, but believe me, everything will work out. You're going to like her."

"If you think that's the problem, you really don't understand."

"Lydia, are you all set?" An older man came into the room. "What's this, Alex?" he teased. "Aren't all the other women in Lindleton enough for you? Now you're after my wife."

Lydia went into her husband's arms, as if for refuge. "I was just trying to get Alex to let me stay and meet Jessica here," she told him.

Alex and the older man, Ben, exchanged concerned looks, but Alex shook his head. "Jessie's been through so much," he said firmly. "I don't know how mature she is now, but even if she's all grown up, she needs things to be calm for a while. Let me have some time with her first."

"He's right," Ben told Lydia. "It'll be easier for her to meet us at the restaurant."

"Mom!" A pretty teenage girl wearing a gold-and-black soccer uniform pushed her face against the front screen door. "I'm going to be late for my game!"

"Come on." Ben held out his hand to his wife. Reluctantly she took it. "We'll see you at the restaurant about five-thirty. Just give us a call if Jessica's late," Ben told Alex.

"I will." Alex followed the couple to the porch and watched them walk hand in hand down the front path to the driveway. When they were gone he settled himself in a wicker chair and stared out at the road. There was nothing to do now except think.

How had he gotten himself into this situation? He had always been fond of Jessica Cassidy, shy little Jessie with the huge brown eyes and the tentative smile. But Jessie was a piece of his past; it had been five years since he had seen her.

The Bancroft family was another matter entirely. They were part of his present and his future because they were part of the little community he now called home. And Ben was his colleague. When Lydia had asked for Alex's help, Alex had not been able to say no.

Now he shifted in his seat and propped his feet against the porch railing. The truth was that he just couldn't let any of them down. Not Jessica, not Lydia, not Ben. He was Alex Grainger, a man who avoided personal involvements the way some people avoided fattening foods. But now he was trapped by his own compassion into playing a role he didn't want. For better or for worse, he was part of an unfolding drama that he could only hope would have a satisfying conclusion for everyone.

He sat quietly contemplating the long blacktop road. Finally, in the distance he saw a car driving slowly and stopping frequently as if its driver was reading mailboxes. Alex looked at his watch and then back out at the car, which had slowed to a stop before turning.

"Welcome to Lindleton, Jessie," he said quietly as he watched the car pull into the Bancrofts' driveway. "May your stay here only bring you happiness." With a sigh, he stood to wait for her.

Chapter One

The small town built on lush, green hills studded with maple, oak and sycamore trees was strange. The house, cut from cinder-gray granite like an ancient gothic cathedral, was strange, too. Only the man leaning against a front porch pillar was familiar.

Jessica Cassidy pulled her Volvo into the tree-lined driveway that led to the stone house, parked in front of a separate garage and switched off the ignition. There was an expectant hush, like the instant before a great symphony plays its first thrilling chord, and then a burst of bird song split the air. Jessica sighed as if she had unconsciously been waiting for the bird's music to help her release the tension that had been building as she neared Lindleton.

It wasn't that she wasn't glad to be there. It wasn't that she wanted to be anywhere else. It was just that coming signaled the beginning of a life that promised only change. Her former life had ended months before with the death of both her parents. Now the time had come to move on.

Through the row of nodding poplars Jessica could see Alex Grainger step off the porch to approach her car. For a moment she experienced the same tremors of excitement that had always racked her body when, as a teenager, she had found herself in his presence. She smiled slightly at her own reaction. She was twenty-two, not sixteen with a hopeless crush on an unattainable Greek god. Now Alex was just a man like many.

Nevertheless, she was glad that she had stopped at the roadside rest area to comb her hair and freshen her makeup. At least she wouldn't be at a disadvantage for this meeting. Quickly she checked her image in the rearview mirror and was reassured by what she saw. Then she opened the door and swung her long legs over the side of the seat, smoothing down the skirt of her cinnamon-colored dress. In a moment she was walking through the trees to greet him.

"Hello, Alex. It's been a long time."

"Jessie?"

The surprise in his voice was a tribute. She gave him a warm smile, the same smile that recently had sent male hearts at the Oberlin Conservatory of Music pounding in double time. If she remembered correctly, the last time Alex had seen that smile, it had been encased in metal and rubber bands and it had represented a year of profit on one of her father's multitude of investments.

"You can't be surprised to see me. You're the one who suggested that I come." Her voice emerged low and husky and exactly the way she had hoped it would.

"I was expecting someone else."

It was the nicest thing that he could have said. Jessica knew precisely whom he had expected: a teenager who had given up hope of ever outgrowing the gawky stage, a shy, sad wallflower who hated her red hair and her coltish legs, a future debutante who would rather hide in the country club powder room than flirt and stalk.

Jessica could pretend to deny it to herself, but she knew that she had come to Lindleton partly for Alex's reaction to the new Jessica. In all the years that she had been growing into her legs and counting the days until her braces came off, she had known that she would not be able to declare herself a complete success until Alex Grainger looked at her just this way. Now she could rest assured that the metamorphosis was complete.

He stepped closer and lifted a strand of the long auburn hair that lay like heavy satin over her shoulder. "And to think," he murmured, "that I used to tease you about this."

"You used to tell me that my hair was exactly the color of the baboons at the Pittsburgh zoo." Jessica examined him with the same frank appraisal he was giving her.

He was still the same wonderful Alex. Better, perhaps, because now his good looks were anything but boyish. They were mature man and more impressive for it. His sandy brown hair waved back from his forehead and over his ears in a peculiarly masculine manner. He had a mustache, new since she had seen him four, no five, years before. It was a glorious effort, thick and long, and she'd bet her life that it was soft to the touch. But nothing about him could eclipse the sparkling green eyes that crinkled when he smiled or laughed. And since he did so much of both, the crinkles were becoming attractive, permanent additions to his face.

Jessica had to look up at him for the examination because although she was tall herself, Alex was that much taller. Tall and broad shouldered and trim enough to promote a health club if he wanted to. She bet he jogged, or swam regularly, or played racquetball. She bet the women in Lindleton fought for the privilege of doing those things with him. And more.

"Just when did you get so pretty?" he asked.

Her brown eyes widened in appreciation at his words. Yes, she was glad she had decided to come. "In my second year of college, I think. I was a late bloomer. Just as I'd given up hope completely, everything came together."

"It sure did." He brushed her cheek with the back of his index finger and then bent the short distance to kiss her in the same place. His mustache placed its own whisper-soft caress on her cheekbone. "Welcome."

"Thank you." Jessica's smile was an outward expression of the emotion rippling through her body. She realized that this day was the first time in a long while that she had felt anything except sadness.

Alex stepped back and continued his assessment as he questioned her. "Did you get to see much of the town?"

Jessica shook her head. "Not really. I got a late

start from Pittsburgh, so I didn't have a chance to look around as I drove through.''

"Was your trip all right?"

"Mercifully short. I can see why you settled here. It's still close enough for you to get back to the city to visit your mother.''

Alex took her arm and they began to stroll toward the house. "I can't tell you how sorry I am about your parents,'' he said, squeezing her arm in a comforting gesture. "I know how difficult this year has been for you.''

Jessica couldn't count how many times in the past months she had been required to respond politely to words of consolation. But this time it was different. She and Alex had grown up together. Her parents had been best friends with his. At times the Cassidys had been surrogates for him when he'd needed another adult to charm or to wheedle a favor from. She knew his sympathy was heartfelt. "I'm starting to put it behind me,'' she said simply. "I know that coming here for the summer will help.''

"I thought it might.'' On the front porch he stopped and motioned to a wicker chair. "Why don't you sit down and rest for a few minutes. Lydia left some lemonade for us.''

"Where are the Bancrofts? I'm looking forward to meeting them.'' Jessica had been so involved in her reunion with Alex that she had almost forgotten her real reason for coming to Lindleton. Now she wanted to meet the family who had asked her to spend the summer months with them as a music tutor.

"Molly had a soccer game, so the whole family went to watch. They're going out to dinner afterward, and we'll join them there." Alex disappeared into the house, giving Jessica a chance to study her surroundings.

The house was located in the midst of acres of unspoiled farmland. It wasn't the posh suburb that she had expected. The neighboring houses were modest and rustic. The Bancrofts' house was the crown jewel; Dr. and Mrs. Bancroft were obviously the landed gentry. The small town of Lindleton seemed remote and inaccessible, but in reality it was close enough to reach in five minutes. The Bancrofts had the best of two worlds. Jessica felt instantly at home, though she had lived in the city all her life.

"Here you go." Alex came out carrying a tray with a pitcher of icy lemonade and a platter of chocolate chip cookies.

Jessica admired the way he moved. He had always had a coiled-spring intensity to his movements that belied his casual manner. She wondered if there was more to Alex than met the eye. It was an intriguing thought. "This is so lovely," she said, gesturing to the landscape. "I feel like I'm in a Thomas Hardy novel."

"The pastoral English countryside?" Alex set the tray down and poured lemonade for both of them. "I know. I think that's why I decided to settle here."

"The Bancrofts ought to have sheep, and we'll have to get the man across the road to trade his chain link fence for stone, but otherwise…"

"You should see it in the winter when it's covered with snow. Northwestern Pennsylvania rivals New England for beauty."

Jessica sipped her lemonade. "So you settled here for the scenic wonders?"

"You sound skeptical." Alex sprawled in his chair, stretching his legs in front of him. Jessica remembered watching him do the same thing when he was eighteen and she was just becoming aware of the male species. Now, as then, she noticed how even in the most relaxed of postures, Alex retained an unaffected poise. She had never seen him at a disadvantage, no matter what the situation.

She drew her attention back to their conversation. "I know people change. But the Alex I knew was a city man."

"I still get to the city every chance I can. Pittsburgh, Cleveland, Toronto. They offer everything I need in the way of urban attractions."

She cocked her head at his words. "Do you have that much time off?"

He grinned and helped himself to a cookie. "You're all grown up, but you haven't changed, Jessie."

It was said with such disarming warmth that Jessica couldn't feel insulted. "Why do you say that?"

"I've never met anyone who tried so hard to make sense out of everything that's said to her. You've always taken every snippet of conversation and milked it for all the information it contained." He took another cookie and handed it to her. "I've always thought it was charming."

"You should have told me that when I was sixteen and needed to feel charming." She ate the cookie, licking the melted chocolate off her fingertips when she was finished.

"And you don't need to feel charming now?"

"Not as badly. But it can't hurt." She leaned back and closed her eyes, letting the peace of her surroundings settle over her. "Tell me about your life here."

Alex was silent so long that she finally opened her eyes and turned a little to find out what was wrong. He was searching her face as though he were looking for some clue that he had not yet found. "Alex?"

He shrugged, and the old familiar grin took over his features. "What do you want to know?"

"Catch me up. Tell me everything."

"Don't tell me my mother didn't keep you informed."

"Only the most mundane details. What's it really been like becoming a doctor? Are you happy? Overworked?" She didn't ask the more personal questions. She knew that he was probably in the middle of a passionate love affair, or about to begin or end one. She hadn't known Alex all her life not to know that much about him.

"Yes to the last two questions. My practice is thriving, I've got more patients than I can realistically cope with, but I haven't gotten to the point where I can say no yet."

Jessica imagined that the warmth of his personality and his keen intelligence appealed to many inhabitants of the town. She was sure his good looks and charming grin didn't hurt, either. Young Dr. Kildare. "And your partner is working out?"

"Very well. Lindleton's so small that there aren't as many specialists as you'd find in larger cities. We see a wide variety of cases we'd never see in Pittsburgh. That's what makes family practice so interesting.''

"And time-consuming."

"That, too."

"And frustrating at times."

Alex grinned. "When you were ten and you'd get too serious, I could always pull a pigtail. What do I do now?"

Jessica smiled back. "I guess we'll have to develop an entirely new way of relating to each other since the pigtails went years ago." Before either of them could probe that possibility, she continued, "Why don't you tell me about the Bancrofts."

"What do you want to know?"

"Enough so that I won't say or do the wrong thing until I've had a chance to feel my way."

"There's nothing you could do that would be wrong. They're really looking forward to having you here for the summer," he reassured her.

When Alex had called her weeks before with the offer of a position teaching the Bancroft children for the summer, Jessica had been skeptical that such a position really existed. She had suspected that Alex, perhaps at his mother's urging, had convinced the Bancrofts to hire her just to get her away from Pittsburgh and a year of sad memories. Staunch denials from Alex's mother—who seemed as surprised as Jessica—and several phone calls from Lydia Bancroft had turned Jessica's skepticism into the conviction that she was really wanted. Perhaps Alex had made the original suggestion, but Jessica no longer doubted that she would be a welcome addition to the Bancrofts' summer plans.

"Tell me what they're like," she asked now.

"Casual, warm, funny."

"They sound wonderful."

"After what you've been through, they'll be perfect for you."

How had he known? Years and miles had separated them, and yet this man, who had never thought of her except as a pesky kid sister—if indeed he thought of her at all—seemed to understand her needs better than anyone else had. "I've been at loose ends since my parents died," she admitted.

"Do you want to talk about it?"

Jessica played with the strands of hair that fell over her shoulder. It was a habit left over from her adolescence, a way of avoiding eye contact when eye contact was too painful. "There's nothing to say, really. My father's death was slow and tragic. Then after my father died, my mother didn't want to live, either. Her death was almost a blessing."

"And you went through it by yourself."

"I was in and out of college. My parents refused to let me drop out completely to take care of them. Both of them had so many friends that there was always someone around to help. And, of course, your mother was a support."

"She understands about grief."

"And now I do, too. But it's over with. My parents are gone. There doesn't seem to be a better place in the world to get started living again than Lindleton."

"May I say one more thing about it before we put it to rest?" Alex asked.

Jessica nodded.

Alex wrapped his legs around his chair and turned

to face her. Jessica was warmed by the empathy on his face. If she was being treated to his bedside manner, she could understand why he was a popular physician.

"I was eight years old when Marion and Robert adopted you. You were just a two-year-old tangle of arms and legs and bright red hair, and I couldn't even begin to imagine what they saw in you. Until then, they'd been like second parents to me. In fact, they were spoiling me so badly that I'm sure it had an effect on my father's decision to arrange your adoption."

Jessica was moved by the emotion in his voice and the gaze that seemed to see right into her heart. This was not the Alex she knew, and for a moment it was almost too much to bear. She tried to inject a lighter note. "Alex, no one else needed to spoil you. Your parents did a fine job of it by themselves."

He ignored her gentle gibe. "I never saw anyone as happy as your parents were. They walked around on air for a month. They had tried for years to have a baby of their own, and they'd given up hope of ever adopting a child because of their ages. When you came they were sure you were a miracle." He reached for her hand and held it. The gesture melted whatever defenses she had erected against his sympathy. He squeezed her hand as he said, "When you think back on your life with Marion and Robert, just remember how it began, not how it ended."

Jessica's eyes filled with tears, and she could only sit quietly for a moment and swallow hard. "Thank you," she managed finally.

"Don't say that again," he admonished with mock

severity. Jessica understood that the intensity of the moment had affected him, too, and he was falling back on humor to get them both through it. It was not often that Alex indulged in serious sentiment. "Maybe my suggestion that you come for the summer will be good for you, but actually I did it for myself. I was busy doing my residency and setting up my practice while you finished growing up, so I got cheated out of seeing the final product. I had to remedy that."

Jessica became conscious that he was still holding her hand. It was a healing gesture, and it was working. No matter what she said about needing to get on with her life, she wasn't sure sometimes that it was possible. Now, holding Alex's hand and letting his warmth infuse her body, she knew hope.

"When do we meet the Bancrofts?"

Alex squeezed her hand again and then pulled his free to examine his watch. "We can go after we get your things inside." He stood and Jessica did, too, following him down the path to her car. In a moment they were both carrying suitcases into the house.

"Lydia's giving you the guest suite on the second floor."

Jessica followed him past numerous rooms and up an elaborately carved walnut staircase. Even though the house was gothic in appearance, it was bright and comfortable inside with well-designed lighting and a casual decor that successfully offset the ponderous stone. Only the fireplaces and an occasional stained-glass window reminded Jessica of an English country manor.

"This is lovely!" Jessica set her suitcase down in

the room that Alex indicated. He followed and stood watching her obvious pleasure. "I didn't expect anything so nice."

"I told you, the Bancrofts are thrilled to have you here."

Jessica walked around the room admiring the antique cherry furniture and the brass bed complete with a white spread that looked as though it were handwoven. She buried her nose in the fresh pink and yellow roses in a crockery pitcher on the dresser. "I feel like an honored guest."

Alex pointed to a door. "There's a private bath through there and a small sitting room on the other side that connects to Molly's room. But you can explore later. We probably ought to leave now."

"Do I have time to see the piano?"

Alex smiled at her request. "We can make time."

Downstairs he led her through the house to a room in the very back. He opened the door and flicked on the light. "Here you go."

"They really are serious about this, aren't they." Jessica hadn't expected a music room. Only the most dedicated or the wealthiest people she knew had such a luxury. This room was a dream come true. Shelves lined one wall piled with volumes of music, instrument cases and musical figurines. Against another wall was a collection of music stands and a case that Jessica imagined contained a guitar. But by far the most impressive feature of the room was the full-sized grand piano that stood in the center.

"A Chickering. A real, old-fashioned, rosewood Chickering." Jessica almost skipped to the piano to let her fingers fall on the ivory keys. She played a few chords and then ran up and down the keyboard in a series of scales. "Listen to that tone quality. I think I'm in love."

"I gather it will do."

"Imagine having this wonderful piano and not wanting to take lessons." Jessica shook her head. "I hope I can change the kids' minds. I've got a degree but not much experience teaching yet."

"Molly shouldn't be a problem. But Clancy might prove difficult. Lydia swears that it's not that they don't like music, it's just that they needed a new teacher. Someone who doesn't think that music ended when Bach passed on." Alex came to stand beside her, resting his arm casually on her shoulders. "I think you'll be able to help."

"I can sure try." For a moment Jessica leaned against him and put her arm around his waist. She liked the feel of his firm muscular body against hers. This was Alex, her not-quite-brother who was proving to be a port in the storm that had been her recent life. She was overwhelmed by gratitude, or another unnamed emotion closely its kin. "I'll have lots of hours in here," she said finally, regretting the separation from Alex more than the separation from the magnificent grand piano.

"We ought to go now."

"I guess we ought to," she echoed.

Neither moved, and then both did, stepping firmly apart. Before Jessica could start toward the door, however, Alex stopped her. "No matter what comes of this summer for you," he said, his green eyes serious, "I just want you to know that I'm glad you've come. And I'll be nearby if you need me. Any time of the day or night.''

"I'm glad, too, Alex," she said, puzzled by the gravity of his expression. She tried to lighten his mood. "Do you make house calls for old friends?"

"Just don't tell my patients if I do."

"It'll be our secret."

"Let's go meet the Bancrofts," he said with a return of his smile.

"I'm ready." With one last look around the room, she followed Alex out the door.

Chapter Two

"The Ale 'n' Cow?" Jessica read the sign over the sprawling, weathered building set in the middle of nowhere. "Someone would actually name a restaurant the Ale 'n' Cow?"

"The proof's right there." Alex pulled his Porsche into an available space and cut the engine. "This is strictly a steak and spaghetti town. If you want gourmet fare, you have to drive back down to Pittsburgh."

"It's not 'gourmet' I'm worried about. Have you ever tried to link the ptomaine poisoning cases that you treat to this restaurant?"

"It was Clancy's choice. All his junior high school friends come here with their parents on Sundays." Alex opened his door and stepped out of the car.

Jessica didn't wait for Alex to come around to help her. She stepped out, too, and followed him through the parking lot. On both sides of the stable-style doors leading into the restaurant were life-size fiberglass

Angus bulls. Alex stopped in front of one and motioned to its nose. "Push it and see what happens."

On closer examination she saw that the nose was actually a round black button. She did as she was told and a sound, somewhere between the moo of a cow in need of milking and the roar of a 747 jet, bellowed through the air.

"And now you know why they call it the Ale 'n' Cow," Alex said with a grin.

"It doesn't sound like it's ailin', it sounds like it's dyin'."

"Don't mention that to the management, they'll change its name to the Dye 'n' Cow, and the food and drink are bad enough already." Alex held the door for her, and Jessica went through.

Inside, the raucous strains of barn dance music drowned out the normal hum of restaurant chatter. Clusters of people circled a salad bar set on the back of another of the preposterous Angus bulls. Waitresses ran back and forth dressed in Annie Oakley costumes complete with six-shooters. The walls were decorated with every kind of Western memorabilia imaginable including Wanted posters of otherwise distinguished-looking men and women.

"The posters are of local politicians," Alex informed her as he guided her toward the back of the room.

"That only makes sense," Jessica agreed politely. "Who else?"

She had been so busy absorbing the absurd atmosphere that for a moment Jessica had forgotten she was about to meet the family that had asked her to come to Lindleton. When a short man with attractive graying hair stood as they approached his table, she was brought back to reality.

"Here we are, Jessie," Alex said softly. His hand tightened on her arm as though he was offering her reassurance.

"This must be Jessica." The man stepped forward. "I'm Ben Bancroft. Welcome to Lindleton."

"Thank you, Dr. Bancroft," she said, offering her hand.

"And this is my wife, Lydia."

Jessica turned to greet the woman seated at his side. Lydia Bancroft was lovely, with chin-length hair and a youthful face that glowed with good health. Her brown eyes were shining with welcome. "I'm so glad you've come," she said softly, extending her hand to Jessica.

Ben Bancroft draped his arm over his wife's shoulders in a gesture that was almost protective. "And this is Molly."

A teenage girl rose from the end of the table and held out her hand to Jessica. "Hi."

"Hi, Molly." Jessica considered the pretty sixteen-year-old who would be even prettier in a few years. Molly was slender with short brown hair the color of Lydia's and enormous brown eyes that almost swallowed her face. Jessica recognized the signs. Molly was going to be a late bloomer, just as Jessica had been. And when Molly filled out and found her own unique style, she would be a real beauty.

"Clancy's around somewhere. He'd much prefer to spend his time with his friends than with his family." Ben said the words with no trace of resentment. Jessica suspected that, like most parents of teenagers,

Ben and Lydia were secretly grateful that their four-teen-year-old son sometimes preferred his peers to them.

Alex pulled out a chair at the end of the table and seated Jessica, then he took the seat next to hers. "Have you ordered yet?" he asked Ben.

"No, we haven't been here long." His words were punctuated by the bleat of a beeper. Ben pressed the button of the small black box that was hooked over his belt and listened to a short message. "Will you excuse me?" he asked. In a moment he was gone.

"Ben's been expecting this call. He's got a patient in the early stages of labor right now," Lydia explained to Jessica.

Jessica knew that Ben Bancroft was the only obstetrician in Lindleton. Although family practice physicians and some general practitioners also delivered babies, Alex had told her on the way to the restaurant that in addition to normal pregnancies, Ben got all the referrals for patients with potentially difficult deliveries. Consequently, Ben rarely had a moment to call his own.

Jessica knew that it wasn't an uncommon scenario. Alex's own father had been an overworked obstetrician who had rarely been home long enough to do more than eat and catch a few hours' sleep. And though Alex had chosen a slightly different path, Jessica suspected that he, too, was busier than any human ought to be. She was glad that he had found the time today to help her get acquainted with the Bancrofts.

"Let's order," Lydia continued. "I know what Ben

wants. If he can't stay, I'll take it home and heat it up for him later.''

Jessica was drawn to the woman with the soft voice and the shining eyes. There was something about Lydia Bancroft that made her feel completely comfortable. Rarely did a stranger look at you with such total acceptance. Again, Jessica was glad that she had come. ''What's good?'' she asked, as she examined the menu.

''Absolutely nothing,'' Lydia apologized. ''But the strip steak is actually tender enough to chew.''

''I just want onion rings!'' A high-pitched male voice reached them at the same time that a gangling young man threw himself into a chair at the opposite end of the table.

''We didn't come to this god-awful place just to order you onion rings, Clancy. You have to have something with protein, too,'' Lydia said calmly.

''Onion rings have protein. They use egg in the batter.''

''How do you know what they use in the batter?'' Molly asked with a snort. ''You probably wouldn't even recognize an egg if you saw one.''

''Find something else to order with your onion rings,'' Lydia interrupted, ''or I'll make you go through the salad bar.''

Jessica watched Clancy's face pucker into a convincing frown as he studied the menu. Clancy had brown hair like his mother and sister, but instead of their brown eyes his were as blue as a summer sky. Despite his frown, he had a face that would never be convincing in anger. Jessica knew that he probably smiled more than most teenagers thought was wise.

He looked up and caught her perusal. "You must be the piano teacher," he said. "I'm Clancy."

"Hello, Clancy. I'm Jessica."

"I'm sorry," Lydia apologized. "Clancy got me so flustered I completely forgot to introduce you."

"I'll have a hot dog with my onion rings." Clancy closed his menu and smiled at Jessica. "I don't want to take piano lessons. I'm going to be a hard case," he said cheerfully.

"I love a good challenge," she answered, not at all offended. Jessica tried to imagine herself at the age of fourteen saying something so wonderfully rude to an adult. She had been brought up by parents who coddled and adored her, but they had also demanded that she be quiet and well behaved at all times. Jessica could see that the wind blew in a completely different direction at the Bancroft house.

"If you love a challenge, you're going to love me," Clancy said.

"Impossible!" Molly muttered.

"Is this frightening you to death?" Lydia asked, reaching across the table to put her hand lightly on Jessica's. "Shall I lie and say that they're just hungry and tired and that they never behave this way at home?"

Jessica pretended to consider. Then she smiled back at Lydia. "You have no idea just how welcome this is."

Was she imagining it, or did Lydia's eyes fill with tears of sympathy? There was a long pause, and then Lydia patted Jessica's hand before she withdrew her own. "You have no idea just how welcome you are," she said cryptically. "In the meantime, if the kids get to be too much for you, let me know and I'll promise to calm them down.''

Ben returned and they ordered.

''How's the patient?'' Alex asked, tilting his chair back.

''Slow. She's a primipara.'' Ben caught the frown on Jessica's face. ''This is her first labor,'' he explained.

''I'm glad that's all. It sounded like a fatal disease.''

''You'll get used to the shop talk,'' Lydia assured her. ''By now I feel as if I could deliver babies myself.''

Alex laughed. ''You probably could. Most deliveries are so routine that doctors aren't really needed.'' As he talked, Alex tunneled his hand under Jessica's hair and rested it on her back to keep his balance. She was suddenly very aware of the casual intimacy between them. It was almost as if five years had vanished, and yet that wasn't quite true. Five years before, Alex wouldn't even have noticed she was sitting beside him.

''You'd better not tell your patients that, Alex,'' Molly said, ''or they'll stop paying you.''

Alex favored her with a grin. ''Who'd hold their hands and pant and blow with them, then?''

''Shouldn't their husbands be doing that?'' Jessica asked.

''You just walked into a trap,'' Clancy said, rolling his eyes. ''Now they're going to talk about their favorite subject.''

Jessica was hooked. ''Husbands?''

''No.'' Lydia shook her head. ''Husbands in the

delivery room. Lindleton General is still in the dark ages. They're absolutely refusing to let husbands witness the birth of their babies.''

''I thought that was done everywhere now.''

''Not here. Last month they finally decided to allow new fathers to come into the recovery room and hold their babies for a minute or two, but that's the closest we've gotten yet.''

''What a shame.'' Jessica turned to Alex. ''How do you feel about that? And you, Dr. Bancroft?''

The older man smiled at her. ''Call me Ben. I think husbands and wives belong together at such an important moment.''

''So do I,'' Alex agreed. ''Ben and I are working hard on getting the hospital board to change. But changes come slowly here. Some of the other physicians in town are adamantly opposed to the idea. Even my partner doesn't like it. He envisions fathers fainting with anxiety in the middle of a difficult delivery.''

''I'd think that if anyone was going to faint it would be the mothers. Especially if they didn't have a loving supporter in the room with them.'' Jessica turned to Alex. ''What do women do who refuse to go along with the system?''

''They drive to one of the bigger cities nearby. Of course if it's the middle of a blizzard or they're having a fast labor, then that's impossible.''

''Some women are choosing to deliver at home,'' Ben added. ''Without medical intervention at all.''

''Not even a midwife?''

''There are several women who help out at home births, but none of them are trained midwives. Luckily they're all willing to call in help if it's needed.

About six months ago we almost lost a mom who had last-minute complications. Fortunately the 'midwife' rushed her to the hospital and saved her life.''

"Enough about that," Lydia said firmly. "Jessica's going to think we're all obsessed."

"No, I'm fascinated."

"Jessie has such good manners that she'd never tell you if she wasn't fascinated," Alex explained.

"Has he always talked to you that way?" Lydia asked, her eyebrow arched in response to Alex's teasing. "How did you put up with him all those years?"

"I developed Alex-defenses." Jessica turned to smile at him, and for a moment she almost forgot that they were surrounded by the Bancroft family. His answering smile was affectionate. His eyes shone with something that was curiously like pride.

"Did you develop Jessica-defenses?" Clancy asked him as the waitress approached with their orders.

"I don't think so," Alex answered, his eyes still locked with Jessica's. "And it's just possible I may live to regret it."

"That was the Bancroft family, condensed, compressed, and capsulized," Alex said afterward, as he helped Jessica back into his car. "What do you think?"

"Well, I was just wondering how I would have turned out if I'd been raised by people like that."

Alex's glance was curious, but he didn't question her until they were roaring down the road into town. During dinner, he had promised her a tour, and now he was fulfilling his promise. "What did you mean," he asked, "about being raised by people like that?"

"Well, they're just so different from my parents. Both Lydia and Ben are so relaxed with the kids. There's so much spontaneity and so much laughter. Ben's so droll and Lydia's so genuinely warm."

"And you can use a dose of warmth and laughter."

"There's never enough of either in the world. I think I'll just soak it up this summer."

"You deserve it."

Jessica watched as the scattered houses got closer and closer together until finally they reached the spot where Lindleton officially began.

"Don't blink, or you'll miss most of the interesting sights," Alex warned, slowing down so that she couldn't possibly miss anything.

"What interesting sights?"

"The ones you just missed when you blinked."

"That bad, huh?"

"Worse. But you're going to learn to love it, anyway." Alex guided the Porsche through the nearly deserted streets. It was a Sunday evening, and Lindleton had its own set of blue laws that no one was energetic enough to challenge. Jessica admired the neatly trimmed lawns planted with flowering shrubs of every size and color. Weeping willow trees nodded gracefully in the light breeze and towering maples guarded the narrow brick avenues like unchallenged sentries.

"This is the main shopping district," Alex said, rolling down his window and flicking off the air conditioner. "You can buy anything you want in Lindleton, providing that you're not picky about color, size or quality."

"I like having my choices made simple." Jessica pointed to a tiny frame building set off by itself on a double lot filled with cars. "What's that?"

"Lindleton's teenage mecca, the Pizza Stop. I think it's set so far from everything else to keep the town fathers from being assaulted by hard rock. Unfortunately the Pizza Stop has the best ice cream in town, so you have to get used to the noise if you have a sweet tooth."

They turned a corner and drove down a street of staid, unpretentious businesses. "There's the post office, and that big brick building with the clock tower is the city hall, the jail, the courthouse and everything else official." After several more blocks Alex pointed to a three-story building. "That's Lindleton General. If you ever need me, that's where you can usually find me. My office is there."

They wove back and forth through the streets until they were close to the center of town again. Alex parked on the edge of a wide grassy park. "This is the town square. When anyone gives you directions, they'll always use this as their point of reference."

"It's very pretty." Jessica got out when she saw that Alex was opening his door and followed him across the tree-dotted square. In the center was a bandstand, designed to resemble a graceful white gazebo.

"They have concerts here, beginning next week. There's a civic orchestra and a chorus, too. They're both pretty good."

"I like the idea of everyone being able to perform

who wants to," Jessica mused. "In the city you have to be top quality to be heard by anyone. The rest of us never get a chance."

"What's this 'us' bit? You're a professional, not an amateur like most of the people who perform here."

"I'm good, Alex, but not brilliant. I've never had any desire to be a concert artist." Jessica sat on one of the green benches under the shade of an oak tree near the bandstand. Alex joined her, sprawling with male grace on the bench.

"Well, what do you want to be when you grow up, then?"

She turned to face him, her hands on her hips until she realized that he was teasing her. His eyes were roaming the soft curves covered by her silky, cinnamon-colored dress, and his face held the approval of a man who knows he's talking to a woman.

"You've got to promise you won't laugh," she answered.

"Have I ever laughed at you?"

"More times than I could possibly remember."

Alex lifted a strand of her hair and tickled her nose with it. "I won't laugh."

Jessica tried to ignore the peculiar feeling in her midsection at his closeness. "I want to open a piano studio somewhere and teach kids to love making music."

"Planning to discover a little Van Cliburn?"

"No, although any teacher'd be pleased to get an exceptional student. It's the other kids I really want to teach. The Clancys of the world who think they hate sitting at a piano." Jessica brushed Alex's hand away. "Are you trying to make me sneeze?"

"You just look so serious. I could see you in fifty years, sitting in an overheated parlor with a big Persian cat and an old upright piano. 'One, two, three... one, two, three,'" he mimicked in an old lady's voice.

"Your stereotype is insulting," she said with no rancor. "I hate cats."

"A French poodle?"

"A Great Dane. I'll teach him to bark when a student plays a wrong note and to eat people who tease me."

"And where will this mythical piano studio be? Is there a young man somewhere who is, at this very moment, making a down payment on the house containing said piano studio?"

Jessica was surprised at the question. She raised her eyes to Alex's and wondered if she'd imagined the note of more than casual interest. His green eyes were smoky and impossible to read. With a sweep of her lashes downward she examined his chest and then brought her eyes back to his face. "Several," she said.

"I'm not at all surprised."

"That's nice to hear," she said, lowering her eyes again.

"How old were you when you learned to flirt like that?" he asked softly. "I know I missed it."

"Old enough to have had some practice." She let her lips curve into a sensuous smile, and then, slowly, ever so slowly, she raised her eyes back to his and lowered one eyelid in a saucy wink. "How am I doing?"

"You're taking my breath away."

"I know you too well to think that's difficult to do."

"You'd better be careful. Sometimes familiarity breeds more than contempt." He reached for her hair again, this time winding the whole long length of it around his hand, pulling her closer as he did. Despite the charged teasing, Jessica was surprised by his move. She couldn't remember Alex spending so much time in touching range before.

"Oh, I think contempt is obviously out of the question," she said in a husky voice.

"That seems to leave us with a whole range of emotions to choose from."

"I've always believed in freedom of choice."

"We have that in common." He bent toward her, and she watched his face edging closer.

If he was expecting her to close her eyes, she surprised him. She was still watching in fascination as his mouth stopped a scant inch from hers. "It's time to take you back to the Bancrofts'," he said.

"All right." Her eyes were still open, and she watched as he hesitated. She could almost feel his reluctance war with his curiosity. Then her eyes closed as his mouth brushed hers. She felt his mustache, soft against her face, and she inhaled the clean scent of his skin. The kiss was not the kiss of a lover, nor was it the kiss of a brother. It was the kiss of a man who wonders if he's doing the right thing.

"I guess I can die happy now," Jessica said when he drew away.

Her words broke the surprising tension that lingered in the air. Alex's face was wreathed in a sudden grin, and he tugged her hair sharply before he loosened his hold on it. "What's that supposed to mean?"

"Well, when I was sixteen, I was sure that all I needed in the world to make my life complete was one kiss from Alex Grainger." Jessica knew the fact that she could admit such a thing was a sign of how much she had grown up.

"I never knew that."

"I'm glad. I'd hate to think you noticed."

"I'll have to give that some thought."

"Don't lose any sleep. That was years ago." Jessica stood and stretched. Her legs felt rubbery, but she certainly didn't want Alex to know that. The kiss, as short and as casual as it had been, had left her feeling strangely shaken. She had expected the kiss to put her relationship with Alex firmly in perspective. Instead it had opened doors of longing that she thought had been permanently locked and sealed.

"I haven't changed in those years, Jessie. But you certainly have."

"Even sisters grow up."

"I don't think we can pretend you're my sister anymore," he said in a voice that left no doubts about his meaning.

"Then we'll be good friends," she said. "That's something we both need."

He didn't answer. He just held out his hand, and she grasped it and let him pull her toward the car.

At the Bancrofts' Alex said a casual good-night and left Jessica to settle into her temporary home. Molly was more than happy to show her the ropes.

"You can have the sitting room all to yourself, if you like," she told Jessica. "I don't mind."

"I'd rather share," Jessica answered. Jessica had invited Molly in while she unpacked, and now the teenager was curled up comfortably on Jessica's bed. "I grew up without a brother or sister. Having you so close will be fun for me."

"Being an only child sounds like fun!"

"Clancy's that annoying?" Jessica disappeared into her closet to get more hangers.

"Clancy's a nerd."

Jessica thought of all the appropriate responses to Molly's statement and then rejected them. "Well, just think," she said cheerfully, "you'll learn how to handle nerds better than anyone else. And believe me, you'll have plenty of chances to put that knowledge to good use later."

Molly giggled. "I never thought of that. Even Clancy has a purpose in life."

"You two sound as though you're having a good time." Lydia poked her head through the open door. "I just wanted to see if you needed anything else, Jessica."

"I've got everything I need, thanks. The room is wonderful."

Lydia continued to stand in the doorway as if she couldn't quite make herself leave. "Did Alex give you a good tour?"

"I think I saw everything there was to see."

"Did Alex show you his house?" Molly asked. "It's the talk of the town."

"It wasn't on the tour. Tell me about it."

"He has a hot tub!" Molly squealed, her brown eyes rapturous. "It's the only one in Lindleton."

"Sounds like Alex." Jessica opened a drawer and began to put nightgowns away.

"Actually the house is an old barn that Alex bought and renovated," Lydia explained.

"An old barn as in horses and cattle?"

"Precisely. It was a landmark in these parts, all that was left of an old homestead that burned to the ground years ago. A developer bought the land and then never did anything with it when the economy changed for the worse up here. Alex bought it for a song. Everyone expected him to build a modern house, but you know Alex."

"Alex has never done anything that anyone expected. He just does what he pleases." Jessica got another armload of clothes from her last suitcase. "It's part of his charm."

"He has plenty of that," Molly chimed in.

Jessica wondered if Molly had succumbed to the universal appeal that Alex held for women, but Molly set her straight immediately.

"At least for an older man," the teenager added with the perspective of youth.

Jessica managed to keep a straight face as she finished arranging her clothes.

"Molly," Lydia said, when she saw that Jessica was finished unpacking, "I'm sure Jessica is exhausted. Let's leave her alone to get a good night's sleep."

Jessica realized that she *was* tired, and she wished both Bancroft females pleasant dreams.

The summer sky had darkened into night when she finally slipped between the sheets. There was no familiar hum of traffic to lull her to sleep, only the sounds of crickets and an occasional bird song. She could hear the murmuring of voices in the hallway and the distant hum of a television set from the first floor.

Family sounds. The noises of home. These were the simple things that she had come to miss most of all in the past months. Now she felt their quiet assurance as she settled in for her first night in Lindleton.

The day had been an unqualified success. She liked the Bancrofts, and she knew that they were glad to have her there. Instinctively she knew that Clancy and Molly would not present any large challenge as music students. And then there was Alex.

Alex Grainger. How many nights as a teenager had she lain awake and dreamed about Alex's arms around her? He was still the stuff from which dreams are made. But there was one overwhelming difference. He was no longer the unattainable Greek god. He was interested in her, although she sensed that he was fighting whatever attraction was developing.

It was unbelievably sweet to have her attractiveness confirmed. But anything else between them would be dangerous. She knew him too well to believe that he would allow a relationship to be serious or permanent. He was still the devil-may-care Alex whom she had known and loved with the blind passion that only a teenager is capable of. And although Jessica was now all grown up, she knew somehow that Alex was still the only man she'd ever met who could spin her safe little world off its axis.

Chapter Three

On her first morning in Lindleton, Jessica lay awake watching the room lighten gradually. There was a bird providing wake-up music outside her window, and from downstairs she could hear the sounds of someone starting a new day. She was filled with energy, and the idea of lying in bed until it was a more polite hour to rise was distasteful.

Instead she rose and showered, washing her hair and combing out the tangles with a wide-toothed comb. It was a difficult job, because her hair hung halfway down her back, but when she was finished drying it, she thought it was probably worth the effort. Years before she had given up hating whichever unknown biological parent had cursed her with red hair, and now she flaunted it, proud of its rich color and silken texture.

She had learned to live with the rest of her, too. The thick dark brows that gave her face an untamed quality, the full mouth that had recently come into fashion, and the warm-toned peach skin that didn't freckle unless she defied nature and stayed out in the sun longer than was healthy. She was just Jessica: shy late bloomer. But now she no longer worried about blooming at all.

Unsure what might be considered appropriate attire for a day at the Bancrofts', she pulled on a pleated green skirt and oxford cloth blouse in a lighter shade of the same green. Although she had taken as much time as possible, it was still only seven when she tiptoed downstairs.

The front door had been thrown open to the cool morning breeze, and Jessica took a deep breath of the fresh country air, untainted by the fumes of carbon monoxide from early morning commuters. When she became aware of the sound of a radio coming from the kitchen, she wandered through the hall to stand in the doorway. Lydia was bustling around the cheerful room humming a Beethoven piano sonata.

"Good morning, Lydia. You're an early riser, too."

"Good morning." Lydia turned to face Jessica and gave her a brilliant smile. Just as she had the day before, Jessica felt the sincerity of her welcome in the Bancroft household. "I'm always up with the first birds," Lydia said.

"Me too. It used to drive my parents crazy."

Lydia frowned a little. "Why?"

"Well, they were both night people, and I wasn't. I'd fall asleep right after dinner, but then I'd be up before the household staff was even on duty."

Lydia turned to the counter and began to mix batter

in a stoneware bowl. "So what would you do while you waited for them?"

"I learned to entertain myself." Jessica sat on a stool at the breakfast bar and watched Lydia. "That's when I got interested in music."

"While your parents were sleeping? Was that to wake them up?"

Jessica laughed. "Maybe at first, but I imagine they set me straight right away. No, I remember when I was just old enough to climb on to our piano bench by myself, I'd sit there while the sun came up and push the piano keys down one by one as quietly as I could."

"Do you still have a light touch?"

"How did you know? My pianissimos are extraordinary. My fortissimos need work."

"You'll like our piano. If you breathe on the keys they'll play." Lydia opened the refrigerator and pulled out a plastic mesh carton of blueberries. She dumped the fruit into the batter.

"I do like it. I tried it yesterday when I first got here. It's a beauty."

"I had one very much like it when I was a little girl," Lydia said, beginning to spoon the batter into muffin tins.

"Do you still play?"

"Yes, but not very well." Lydia stopped and leaned on the counter, and for a moment her eyes took on a faraway look as she confronted her past. "When I was younger than you are, I wanted to study to be a concert artist." She stopped for a moment. "Then...well, things just got in the way. By the time I had the leisure to study again I'd lost the drive."

"But you still enjoy it?"

"I especially enjoy listening to others play. I'd like it very much if you'd play something for me later."

Jessica considered Lydia's request. "Well, I'll be happy to, but—and I'm not just saying this—I was cut out to be a teacher, not a performer."

"I'd still like to hear you." Lydia put the muffins in the oven and set the timer. She got eggs from the refrigerator and began to crack them into a bowl for scrambling.

"Tell me about Molly's and Clancy's training."

"First, would you tell me a little more about you?" Lydia was beating the eggs with a whip, and Jessica watched the fluffy yellow liquid swirl around the bowl. "We're so delighted to have you here that I want to get to know you better right away."

Jessica was warmed by the request. It wasn't often that she was given such an open invitation to talk about herself. She sensed that Lydia was really interested. "What would you like to know?"

Lydia smiled. "Whatever you'd like to tell me about."

The subject of her parents was still too sensitive for casual conversation, so Jessica chose her years at Oberlin. She talked about her classes and the friends she had made. Lydia listened with occasional questions and nods of understanding.

"So I realized," Jessica said, finishing her discourse, "that I was fascinated with how people learn and how important it is to set the right environment for study. My roommate wasn't a music major, so I began teaching her piano as an experiment. I found that I was looking forward to that hour each week more than to anything else I was doing. That's when I realized I was born to teach.''

"I'm glad you realized it. Because that's what brought you here." Lydia rescued the muffins and set them on top of the stove. "Will you play for me now?"

It seemed to mean so much to Lydia that Jessica followed her new friend into the music room and seated herself at the piano. "What would you like to hear? Schubert, Bach, Beethoven, Debussy?"

"Debussy."

Jessica began the first Arabesque, a dreamy, impressionistic piece with delicate shading and gentle melody.

"I knew you'd play Debussy well after what you said about your touch," Lydia said. Her voice was husky with pleasure. "Will you play me something else?"

"Do you like Brahms?"

"Very much."

This time Jessica played the Intermezzo in E-flat Major.

"I've always loved the Intermezzi," Lydia said when she was finished. "Especially that one. It sounds almost like a folk song, so simple and yet so complex. You play beautifully, Jessica. One more?"

Jessica felt sufficiently warmed up to tackle something more difficult. "Do you like the darker Brahms works? I played all the Ballades at my senior recital. This one's not performed very often, but I love it. It's the third one in Opus 10. The B Major." After a deep breath she began with a crashing percussive fifth in the bass. The piece was technically difficult, and she was swept along with its beauty and passion until she reached the more legato middle section. Then she played the delicate melody in the piano's upper range with innate subtlety of feeling, finally finishing with a return to the passion of the beginning.

"It almost sounds like Bartók, doesn't it?" she said, when she was finished and breathing easily again.

There was no answer, and she swiveled to see Lydia wiping tears off her cheeks. Jessica turned back to the keyboard and began to play the second Debussy Arabesque to give Lydia time to recover. She could understand the older woman's response. Brahms had always affected Jessica in the same way. When she finished, Lydia was standing behind the piano bench, and she put her hand on Jessica's shoulder.

"This meant more to me than you know." Lydia brushed Jessica's hair back and bent to give her a kiss on the cheek. "Thank you for being here."

At breakfast Jessica began to piece together the Bancrofts' routine. It was simple, really. There wasn't one. In the summertime at least, the Bancroft household was strictly laissez-faire. Clancy and Molly straggled in at different times and cooked their own eggs while Lydia and Jessica read the *Lindleton Courier* and polished off a pot of coffee between them. Lydia had already informed Jessica that Ben had gone to the hospital well before dawn to wait for the arrival of the stubborn baby he had received the phone call about at the Ale 'n' Cow.

"You can never count on Daddy being home," Molly told Jessica. "But when he is, we just take advantage of him as much as we can." Molly straightened a faded Lindleton High School T-shirt and tucked it into her jeans before she sat down to her omelet. Jessica had discovered right away that no one got dressed up in the Bancroft household. Even Lydia was informality personified.

"What she means is that when Daddy's home, we don't work. And that means no piano lessons," Clancy said, his mouth filled with a blueberry muffin.

"Clancy, did you really think I intended to teach you day and night without a break?" Jessica teased. "Nobody learns well that way."

"Old Mrs. Trover sure didn't think that was true. She'd have taught us right around the clock if she could've gotten away with it." Clancy mimicked his previous teacher, sounding so much like Alex's imitation of the evening before that Jessica was sputtering with laughter when he was finished. "One, two, three...one, two, three. That's not right, Benjamin Clancy Bancroft. It's threes, not fours. Oh, my! What will I do with you? We've been on this piece for sixteen hours today, and you still can't get it right. Your poor mother is throwing her money down the drain. One, two, three..."

"She was not that bad," Molly admonished him.

"What happened to poor Mrs. Trover?" Jessica wanted to know, when she could be serious again.

"She retired to Florida," Lydia said, frowning at her son.

Clancy ignored his mother's signal. "She's probably down there right now teaching the sea gulls to caw in threes. Caw, caw, caw...caw, caw, caw..."

"That's enough." Lydia caught Jessica's eye. "If

you think he's impossible, I'll understand. You could just concentrate on Molly for the summer."

"Can this be happening?" Clancy asked, his hand over his chest to fend off an imaginary heart attack. "Could I be this lucky?"

"No, you couldn't!" Jessica squelched his enthusiasm. "The worse you are, Clancy, the more I'm going to like it. I told you yesterday, I love a challenge. Love it! And I'm so excited you're going to provide me with one, I can hardly wait to get started."

"You'll grow old before your time," he warned.

"Then I can help Mrs. Trover teach the sea gulls," she said firmly. "In the meantime, you and I are going to be an item."

"Score one for Jessica," Molly said with a grin.

Surprisingly, the piano lessons went well. Molly seemed to enjoy playing, and she showed a natural musicality that Jessica knew she would be able to help her develop. Molly at sixteen was a romantic. Lost in her own emerging feelings she romanticized everything around her, including pieces that weren't romantic at all. Jessica remembered being sixteen, and she decided to assign Molly a Chopin Prelude that she knew would appeal to her. To tantalize her, Jessica played it through first. Just as she had thought, Molly was hooked, and the rest of the day's lesson was spent working out the most difficult parts.

Clancy, despite everything he had said, was anxious to show off. He played with a crisp, sure touch and perfect hand position. Although he needed help with rhythm—one, two, three...one, two three, in the style of Mrs. Trover—he had an excellent ear for his other mistakes. Jessica realized that she was working with a genuinely talented student.

"Have you had any Joplin yet?" she asked when he was done.

"Is he one of the Rolling Stones?"

"That's Jagger. And you can have some of him, too, if you want. But Joplin's late-nineteenth-century jazz. Ever hear of ragtime?"

Clancy played a few measures of "Frankie and Johnnie." "Like that?"

"Nope." Jessica sat next to him. "Move over. Does this sound familiar?" She began the theme from "The Entertainer."

"I saw that movie on television. *The Sting.*"

"Right." She stopped and then began "Maple Leaf Rag." "Joplin used to play the piano in a saloon in Missouri named the Maple Leaf Club. That's where he began to write music."

"That's neat."

"You have to be able to count," Jessica warned him.

"At least it's not in threes."

Jessica thought the fact that he had noticed it wasn't was just one more sign that Clancy had talent. "Do you want to learn some Joplin?" she asked.

"What about Jagger?" Clancy wasn't giving up easily. "Or Joel, or Springsteen?"

"I'm a Billy Joel fan, too," she said. "If you pick out the melodies in the keys I tell you to, I'll teach you how to put chords with them. That way you'll be able to play anything you want without having to rely on sheet music."

"I already know 'Uptown Girl.'" He began to play

the melody with both hands, occasionally harmonizing with the left.

"Terrific. We'll start on that tomorrow. In the meantime I'll get you some Scott Joplin to work on, too."

"Are we done yet?"

"We're done." Jessica stood. She played her last card. "After dinner I thought I'd go into town and get the music. Maybe you and Molly would come with me and show me where to get ice cream. I'm afraid I'm addicted to chocolate chip."

"I guess I could come." Clancy halted his retreat. "If you're trying to bribe me, Jessica, it just might work." He flashed her a big grin and disappeared through the music room door.

Jessica spent the rest of the day writing letters and taking a long walk to get acquainted with the neighborhood. After months that had revolved around illness and the details of settling her parents' estates, she found the free time was a welcome change. Ben was home by dinnertime and he regaled them all with tales of the delivery of not one but two Lindleton babies who had decided to be born at exactly the same time.

It was only when she was driving toward town with Clancy and Molly in tow that Jessica realized she had missed Alex. Years had gone by without seeing him or thinking of him, but after one afternoon and evening spent in his presence, she already wished that she could tell him the details of her day and find out about his. She refused to dwell on the kiss in the town square, but she knew it remained somewhere in her consciousness, fueling a fire that should have been doused long ago. Jessica tried to pass off her fascination with Alex as loneliness in a new town, but as Clancy and Molly chattered away, she realized that loneliness was not going to be a problem in Lindleton.

"There's the music store!" Clancy shrieked. "Stop!"

Jessica obediently pulled over and got out in front of a shop that seemed to sell everything from air conditioners to xylophones. Inside she found one copy of the sheet music for "Maple Leaf Rag" and ordered *The Collected Works of Scott Joplin* for the future.

"Where to?" she asked innocently when they were back outside.

"Pizza Stop," Molly and Clancy said together, and in a minute they were standing in front of the frame building Alex had pointed out the day before.

Inside, Jessica was the oldest person in the restaurant with the exception of the deaf old man who stood behind the counter flipping pizzas. Wishing she had earplugs, she followed Clancy and Molly to a table by the window where they immediately installed and abandoned her before she even had a chance to protest.

Her own adolescence had been so sedate, and so much of her college time had been spent traveling between school and home and caring for parents, that the Pizza Stop was a revelation for Jessica. She sat by the window idly stirring the bowl of ice cream that had been set down in front of her and watched the antics of the resident teenagers. At first Molly and Clancy had drifted from group to group, but Clancy had finally pulled up a chair at a table of boys his own age.

Molly had just started back toward Jessica when a young man came through the door. Jessica didn't have to be psychic to tell that Molly had expected him. Without so much as a greeting, the young man took Molly's hand and led her to a booth. Once there, they had a whispered conversation, with lots of pointing to Jessica, and finally they got up and came to her table.

"Jessica, meet Mike. Mike, Jessica Cassidy."

Mike was just a little taller than Molly, and he was good-looking in a clean-cut, all-American fashion. Although a number of the teenagers at the Pizza Stop had outrageous haircuts and look-at-me clothes, Mike was dressed in a new pair of blue jeans and a conservative shirt much like Jessica's own. He was friendly, well mannered and obviously anxious to be alone with Molly.

"Would you mind if Mike and I went for a walk?" Molly asked. Her eyes pleaded with Jessica to understand.

"Not at all. But I think you ought to be back in half an hour so I can get you home before your mother worries." Jessica watched them leave and wondered why Molly had looked so grateful for such a small favor.

Jessica was finishing her ice cream when she looked up to see Alex and a petite blonde wearing a nurse's uniform come through the front door. She was torn between being glad to see two more adults and an unexpected stab of jealousy at seeing Alex with another woman. It was just one more warning that her interest in him was reaching the danger zone. Before she could force her feelings into perspective, how-

ever, Alex linked his arm through the nurse's and
brought her to Jessica's table.

"Well, hi," he said, pulling out a chair. "May we
join you?"

Jessica nodded and commanded herself to smile at
Alex's companion. The young woman was attractive
in a perky, too-cute-to-even-be-a-cheerleader way.
Without trying to be cruel, Jessica thought of county
fairs and Kewpie dolls.

"Hi, Jessica," the nurse, whose name was Debby
Greene, said in a deep Lauren Bacall voice that was
at odds with her Kewpie doll image. "Welcome to
our town."

"Thank you." Jessica watched as Alex and Debby
decided between raspberry sherbet and chocolate marble ice cream. The process gave her time to school
her emotions. By the time they settled on the chocolate marble, Jessica was sure she was under control.

"Jessie, unlike a singles bar, this is not the best
place to survey Lindleton's male population," Alex
said as Debby began on her ice cream. "Unless you
like them young."

"I'm here with Clancy and Molly."

"I don't see them."

A few minutes before, Clancy had finished his ice
cream and with Jessica's permission had gone to the
newsstand with his friends to buy a magazine. Jessica
pretended to look around. "How will Lydia feel when
I tell her I lost them in the crowd at the Pizza Stop?"

"Worse than you might think. She's very protective."

Jessica was surprised at Alex's serious tone.
"Clancy's at the newsstand, and Molly's taking a

walk with a very nice boy named Mike," she explained.

"You blundered into something there, Jessica." Before she could ask him what he meant, Alex turned to Debby. "How's your ice cream?"

"Just the way I like it. Cold and loaded with calories." Debby eyed Jessica's slender figure. "I'll bet you don't even have to worry about that, do you?"

Jessica shrugged. "I don't worry about it. Whether I should remains to be seen."

"Jessica's always been skinny," Alex said in an aside to Debby. "She cultivates it."

"Have you two known each other long?" Debby asked, her eyes gleaming with the new piece of information.

"Forever," Alex said solemnly.

"Then you can tell me about Alex's childhood," Debby crowed.

"Where would you like me to start?" Jessica asked. "I know all there is to know."

"Start where he discovered girls."

"Now wait just a minute," Alex began.

"It's okay, Alex," Jessica soothed him. "I realize I was only three, but I still remember loads."

"How old was he?" Debby was entranced.

"Nine. He fell in love with the lifeguard at the country club pool."

"You weren't old enough to remember that," Alex pointed out with a grin. "You were just out of diapers."

"Ah, yes, but I remember my parents talking about it. You used to trail around behind this lifeguard, who

I distinctly remember hearing, always wore a bikini whether she was on duty or not.''

Alex reminisced. ''A lime green bikini with a little bow right in the middle of...'' He stopped and pulled himself back to the present. ''How interesting can this be?''

''He started that young?'' Debby teased.

''It's entirely possible he started even younger,'' Jessica said with a frown, ''but I wasn't around to record it for posterity.''

''Tell me more.'' Debby was almost panting.

''Well, when he was fourteen...'' She stopped and turned to Alex. He was watching her with a half grin, his eyes warm. ''Was the crush on your French teacher when you were fourteen or fifteen?''

''You're doing fine without me.''

''When he was fourteen,'' she began again, turning back to Debby, ''Alex fell in love with his French teacher, who was straight off the plane from Paree. She was about one hundred years old and she had a wart on her nose—''

''It was a mole,'' Alex interrupted.

''A mole on her nose, but Alex loved her accent. That was the beginning of Alex's tendency to fall for every woman who has even one acceptable attribute. Of course the more attributes the better,'' she hastened to add, in case Debby felt that Jessica was making fun of her.

''Do you have the picture now?'' Alex asked dryly. ''Or must Jessica list every woman I've ever lusted after?''

''None of this is new information,'' Debby told Jessica, ignoring Alex completely. ''I could tell you stories about the women he's fallen in love with in Lindleton. Alex is a notorious love 'em and leave 'em kind of guy.''

"Do you suppose Lindleton is large enough for him?" Jessica asked with a completely serious face. "How many women can there be here?"

"Well, you have to remember he's pretty busy with his practice, so that cuts down on his time."

"But how many of his patients are single?" Jessica continued.

"If you ladies are finished tearing my innocent reputation to shreds…" Alex had finished his ice cream, and he was leaning back in his chair.

"Are we finished?" Jessica asked Debby.

"I might consider asking you to come as the guest speaker for our Nurses' Association Dinner next month. The subject being Alex, of course. The rest can wait till then." Debby looked at her watch and stood. "Sorry I have to run off, but Harry's going bowling tonight and I want to see him before he leaves." She leaned over and gave Alex a kiss on the cheek. "Nice to have met you, Jessica."

"Who's Harry?" Jessica asked after Debby had disappeared through the door.

"Debby's husband." Alex had a sardonic smile on his face as he watched for Jessica's reaction.

"I see." She smiled brightly.

"And you're not surprised that she's married, are you?"

"I knew it all the time."

"You thought she was my current love interest."

"She wasn't wearing a wedding ring," Jessica defended herself.

"She doesn't like to work in one. She thinks it's unsanitary."

Jessica lifted her shoulders. "Alex, your love life is none of my business, but knowing you as well as I do, I'll confess I jumped to conclusions."

"You realize, of course, that Debby was probably jumping to conclusions about you, too. Especially after your remarkable insights into my libido."

Jessica considered his statement. If Alex expected her to coyly apologize, he was mistaken. "Do you suppose this is going to set you back a night or two in your search for the perfect woman?"

"At least."

"Think of all the sleep you'll get." She widened her eyes. "You'll be a new Alex by the time the rumors have died down."

"According to your theories, there are a number of women in Lindleton who didn't think there was anything wrong with the old Alex."

"What do they know?" Jessica covered one of Alex's hands in a comforting gesture. She was enjoying their teasing. It was a safe way to relate to him. "Besides, your reputation will be as good as new in a few days. Just treat me the way you always have and no one could possibly believe that there's anything between us. Look—" she held out a handful of her hair "—I'll even put this in pigtails for a week and you can pull them every time you see me. It'll be like old times."

"Except for one thing," he said, pulling the hair from her hand and letting it fall back over her shoulder. "It doesn't feel like old times. Does it, Jessie?"

Her repertoire of teasing replies seemed suddenly

to have gone dry along with her mouth. Rather than stumble over an answer, she said nothing at all. Alex could still tie her tongue with one casually flirtatious remark.

Alex smoothed her hair and then sat back. "I want to talk to you about Molly while we have the chance," he said, changing the subject.

Jessica was grateful for the diversion, and she nodded. "What did you mean earlier about me blundering into something?"

"I was talking about Molly's relationship with Mike. She's crazy about him, and evidently the feeling is mutual. The problem is Lydia. She's very protective." Alex seemed to be feeling his way. "Lydia is adamant that Molly not get involved with one boy. It's not that she doesn't like Mike, it's just that she doesn't want Molly to get serious about anyone."

"But Mike seems so nice. He's polite, and..."

"He could be Mr. Clean and Lydia wouldn't approve."

"So Molly's not allowed to see him?"

"I don't know the whole story, but from what I understand, Molly began to date Mike last fall. Everything was fine until it looked like it was getting to be a steady relationship. Lydia just refused to let Molly see him after that. Now Molly is crushed, Ben is right in the middle, and Lydia is unable to discuss it rationally."

"So when I told Molly she and Mike could go for a walk, that was a major mistake."

Alex nodded. "I think you should try very hard not to get involved in this, Jessie."

"I don't want to get involved, but living right there

and working so closely with Molly, it's going to be tough.'' Jessica tapped her fingers on the table as she thought about Alex's words. "Well, thank you for letting me know what was going on. I'll just have to deal with it the best way I can."

"I know you'll do fine." Alex stood. "I haven't even gone home from work yet. I think I'm going to call it a night."

Jessica wanted to admonish him for not taking better care of himself, but she stopped herself. Telling a doctor to eat nutritious food and get more rest seemed the ultimate in absurdity. Besides, why did it matter to her? "It was nice to see you, Alex," she said instead.

"I'll see you again soon." He walked to the door, stopping to talk to several teenagers before he went out.

Jessica wondered if he had meant his words as anything more than a polite farewell. She really wasn't sure she wanted to see Alex Grainger again soon. When she was alone, she could make herself believe that a relationship with him would be fatally complicated. When she was with him, she couldn't seem to make herself believe anything at all.

From her window she watched as he walked to his car. She admired the confident loose-limbed swing that emphasized his tall, broad-shouldered physique. Jessica was sure that it was just one of the many things that attracted women to him in the first place.

Alex was one of those men who had been given everything that most women find arousing. Looks, personality, intelligence, sensitivity. Alex had them all and he had never minded using them. Debby's teasing words were a warning. Jessica had suspected that Alex hadn't changed; Debby had confirmed it.

"You're the same old devil-may-care Alex, and underneath the new facade, I'm still the same old serious Jessie," Jessica whispered as she watched him climb into the front seat of the Porsche and drive away. "No matter how much I wish it weren't so, you and I are still just as different as we ever were."

Chapter Four

"Bravo, Clancy." Jessica stood and applauded, and Clancy, with the serenity of an artist who knows he has just performed at his top capacity, rose from the piano bench and bowed.

"It was nothing," he said modestly.

"That's not true," Lydia said, clapping loudly. "I've never heard you play like that. It was wonderful."

"That was good, son," Ben said. "See what happens when you put your mind to something?"

"Jessica put her mind to something. I just went along with it. Unless you want to hear my B Major scales and arpeggios, I'm finished." Without waiting for an answer, Clancy favored them all with a pleased grin and left the music room.

"He may not admit it," Lydia told Jessica, "but he's enjoying his lessons with you. He never worked this hard before. Molly's complaining because he's at the piano so much."

"They're both doing well. You've got two talented children."

Two weeks had passed since Jessica had come to Lindleton. During those weeks she had worked hard with both of the Bancroft teenagers, giving formal lessons every other day and helping with their practicing in between if they needed it. In addition, Ben, who was the only family member who knew nothing about music, had decided that he wanted piano lessons. On the rare occasions that he had free time, Jessica had begun to instruct him, too.

"When do I give my first concert?" Ben asked her now as Lydia and Jessica went into the kitchen to finish afterdinner cleanup.

"Anytime you want. You've about mastered 'My Uncle Fred.'"

"That's one concert I don't want to miss," Lydia said, giving her husband a spontaneous hug and kiss.

Jessica turned away, pleasantly embarrassed by the show of affection. She had grown up in a family in which hugs and kisses were private affairs. She liked this better, but it was still something that was hard to get used to.

She began to scrape and rinse the dinner plates and stack them in the dishwasher. It had taken Lydia a full week to agree to let Jessica help with some of the household chores. Now they had developed an afterdinner ritual. Jessica enjoyed it because it gave her a chance to talk with Lydia, who had fast become more than just Clancy's and Molly's mother.

"Ben's having such a good time with his music," Lydia said after he had left. "He's never had time for a hobby. And even if he had, who'd want to teach a fumble-fingered obstetrician who might have to leave in the middle of a lesson to deliver a baby?''

Jessica laughed at Lydia's characterization of the husband she obviously adored. ''He's actually doing well. The hardest part about teaching an adult is that they always know what they're doing wrong. It bothers them that they can't make their fingers behave the very first time they sit down at a keyboard.''

''You're so patient with him. Ben and the kids are crazy about you.'' Lydia's tone left no doubt that she was also pleased with Jessica.

''I'm crazy about them, too.'' Jessica began to rinse glasses and silverware. ''I never had a brother or a sister, and I always wanted one. If I'd been that lucky, I'd have wanted them to be like Clancy and Molly.''

Lydia was quiet for a few minutes. It was obvious from her words, however, that she had been thinking about Jessica's statement. ''I don't mean to pry,'' she said finally, ''but sometimes when you talk about yourself, I get the feeling that you were lonely as a child.''

''I think I was.'' Jessica tried to find the right words to explain. ''You see, my parents were older than most parents are. I was an adopted child, and they were in their late forties when I was placed with them. They were used to a different life-style, and they didn't even have nine months to prepare. One day they were childless with no hope of ever becoming parents, and the next day they were trying to comfort a desolate two-year-old who wanted her mommy.''

"Surely you can't remember that!" Lydia's voice cracked.

"I'm sorry, I didn't mean to make it sound so melodramatic." Jessica had never met anyone as maternal as Lydia. She knew that the picture she was painting would be hard for Lydia to bear. She was so fiercely protective of Molly and Clancy.

"It just makes me so sad," Lydia said, her voice not completely under control.

"My parents were wonderful people," Jessica reassured her. "They dedicated themselves to making me happy. My father was a successful stockbroker, but every night he'd come into the nursery and sit on the floor with me and build elaborate houses of blocks so that I could knock them down. My mother had a social calendar that was extraordinarily complex, but she refused to leave me at home with the staff if she didn't have to. I went to teas and meetings and fundraisers right along with Pittsburgh's elite. By the time I was four, I had better manners than most debutantes do after finishing school."

"They must have loved you."

"They did. And I loved them. I'll always miss them."

"I know you will." Lydia seemed calmer, as if hearing the happy ending of Jessica's story relieved her sadness. "You said that you were two when they adopted you. I'm sure that made the adjustment more difficult."

"I suppose it did. I was old enough to realize that my life had changed, but not old enough to understand why."

"Do you remember your birth mother at all?"

Jessica smiled a little. "You're obviously well-read on the adoptive triangle. Anyone else would have called her my 'natural mother' as if being an adoptive parent is unnatural."

"I have done some reading," Lydia admitted. "It's always interested me."

"I don't have any real memories. Just vague impressions. I remember being held and rocked. I remember wanting her when she wasn't there anymore."

"I'm sorry," Lydia apologized, her voice sad again.

"It's okay. It feels good to talk about it. I never have before."

"Have you ever tried to trace your mother?"

Jessica began to scrub the sink. Lydia had finished putting everything away, and she was standing at the counter watching Jessica. "No, I never have. It would have upset my parents. My birth mother was young and unmarried, and she lived in Pittsburgh when I was born. That's all I know for sure. My parents told me that she was a very sweet girl who couldn't give me the kind of life I deserved. They said she loved me enough to want a better life for me."

"I know she loved you very much," Lydia assured her, her eyes bright with unshed tears. "How could she have helped herself?"

"Thank you," Jessica said. She turned to face Lydia. She was warmed by Lydia's obvious concern. "Did you know that Alex's father arranged my adoption?"

"Yes, he told me."

"Our parents were friends, and of course Alex's

father was an obstetrician. He delivered me, and then, evidently, he stayed in touch with my birth mother. When she decided to give me up, she went to him and asked him to arrange it. I always thought that someday I'd ask him for more information, but he died about four years ago. I suppose it's better this way. My mother has a new life now, and so do I.''

"She might want to get in touch with you."

Jessica considered Lydia's words. "Well, there are organizations where I could register. If both parent and child want to be reunited, they're put in touch. Someday, when I'm ready, I might do that."

"Is it possible that Alex might know something?"

Jessica smiled. "Are we talking about the same man?"

Lydia smiled, too. "Maybe Alex is more serious than you think he is."

"There are two things that Alex is serious about. His practice and his women. I'm not sure that anything else penetrates."

"So you've noticed that Alex is a flirt." Lydia pulled a dish towel off the refrigerator door handle and threw it to Jessica.

"Were you afraid that I hadn't?" Jessica dried her hands.

"I was hoping you understood his basic nature."

"I've known him all my life. I've watched that basic nature take shape. You don't have to worry." Jessica was reassured by her own confident tone. Although she hadn't seen Alex for more than a minute or two in the past two weeks, there had been times when Jessica had wondered if she was as firm on the subject of Alex Grainger as she ought to be.

"It's so easy to make mistakes at your age," Lydia said in a voice that could have doubled for a sigh.

"May I ask you something?"

"Of course."

Jessica tried to phrase her question tactfully. "Are you afraid that Molly's going to make a mistake? Is that why you're not letting her see Mike?"

"Evidently she's been talking to you."

"We spend a lot of time together." Jessica didn't add that the subject of Mike Dempsey came up at least three times a day.

"I imagine I seem overprotective."

"If I say yes, will you send me packing?"

Lydia's smile was genuine. "There's nothing you could do or say to make me send you packing."

"Then yes, I think you're being too protective. But I've never been a mother, have I?"

"No, dear. But when you are, I hope you can come to me and benefit from the wisdom I've gleaned after all the mistakes I've made. In the meantime, I just have to do what seems right."

"No matter what, I think Clancy and Molly are very lucky," Jessica said, reaching out to take Lydia's hand and squeeze it.

"I'm the lucky one, Jessica. I have wonderful children."

Jessica spent the next morning helping Molly paint her bedroom. Since it was a Saturday and Ben was home, lessons had been called off and they were all doing exactly what they pleased. Jessica, whose bedroom at home had always been a sedate, unassuming white, was delighted to help Molly slap bright gold paint on walls that had formerly been deep rose.

"How are you going to sleep in here?" Jessica asked, cocking her head to get the effect of the new color. The walls seemed to undulate in bright waves.

"I'll cover it up with posters," Molly answered, unconcerned.

"Then why are we doing this?"

"So I'll know it's there."

Jessica was still trying to figure out Molly's answer when Clancy came in to tell her that Alex was downstairs.

"Go ahead," Molly told her. "I'll finish it. I think I'm going to paint the trim black."

Jessica was delighted to escape. Without changing out of cutoffs and a faded, paint-spattered T-shirt that had once belonged to Molly, she ran down the stairs.

"Who's this?" Alex asked, as she came into the kitchen to find him. "Not the formal Miss Jessica Cassidy?"

"The one and only," she said.

He stood and lifted a cap that she had borrowed from Clancy off her head. Her hair, which had been tucked beneath, tumbled down around her shoulders.

"Ah, yes. Now I recognize you."

"And you are simultaneously bowled over by my beauty," she prompted him.

"And I am simultaneously bowled over by how grubby you are."

"I probably do need a shower," she admitted, wrinkling her nose as she realized that she was covered with tiny speckles of gold paint.

Alex didn't look grubby at all. He was dressed in

a bright green polo shirt that made his eyes look like emeralds. Someone had obviously told him that green was his color, and he had taken them seriously. He was more gorgeous than usual, and harder to resist pining over.

"How fast can you get cleaned up?" he asked her. "I'd like you to come to a party with me."

She considered his invitation. An afternoon with Alex seemed too good to be true. It also seemed too dangerous. "What kind of a party?"

"A friend of mine has a summer house on Conneaut Lake in Crawford County, and he's invited me there for a barbecue. I'm on call so I wasn't expecting to be able to go, but my partner's going to cover for me until I come back." Alex lifted a strand of bright auburn hair and pretended to inspect it. "You don't even have to wash your hair," he told her. "You managed to keep it out of the paint."

"What should I wear?"

"Something appealing. There'll be lots of young men there for you to meet."

Jessica could not believe what she'd just heard. "Let me see if I have this right, Alex. You're inviting me to come with you so that I can meet lots of young men? Since when have you become my dating service?"

"I feel responsible for you. I brought you up here, and I want to be sure you get a chance to meet some eligible locals."

Jessica swallowed the angry response that promised to put an end to their friendship. She stood in front of him, considering how to answer without giving herself away. It was just possible that she could show

Alex how idiotic his suggestion was. And showing was always better than telling. "Well, fine, Alex," she said in a voice sweet enough to attract a hive of bees. "How thoughtful of you. Let me go change."

In her room she surveyed her wardrobe. She had always chosen classic clothing in the style that was now called "preppy." Hanging in the closet, however, were several impulsive mistakes that she had seldom had the courage to wear. One of them just might do. She pulled out a bright turquoise halter-and-pants set made of raw silk and held it up to examine it. The halter was demure enough in front, but it plunged down to the middle of her spine in the back. It was short enough to leave a tantalizing band of skin bare around her slim waist. The pants, which ended midcalf, fitted snugly and emphasized her long legs.

She showered and dressed, then pulled her long hair into a ponytail high on one side of her face. She applied subtle makeup and perfume and attached dangling chain earrings. The effect was just what she wanted.

"Molly, will you come here a minute?" she yelled through their sitting room. "What do you think?" she asked, when the teenager appeared, a paintbrush in hand.

"Just don't let my mom see you or she'll make you change," Molly said with a giggle.

"I'll sneak out the back," Jessica promised.

Downstairs she found Alex in the living room with Ben. "I'm ready," she said, pretending that nothing was different at all.

Both men gave simultaneous low whistles.

"I didn't mean that appealing," Alex said later as he helped her into his car. "I wasn't asking you to seduce every young man at the party."

On a whim she reached up and put her arms around his neck, pulling him down to kiss his cheek. "You don't have to worry about me," she said in a husky voice. "I'll be just fine."

The drive was leisurely as if Alex was deliberately holding the powerful Porsche in check on the almost deserted country roads. Jessica sat back, a faint smile on her lips as she watched the scenery unfold. Forty-five minutes later they crossed the Crawford County line. Beyond the barest formalities, they had hardly exchanged a word.

Alex's friend lived on the east shore of Conneaut Lake in a rambling, two-story frame house that had been painted drab olive. The front, facing the lake, was a huge glassed-in porch, and there, Alex began to introduce Jessica to the other party-goers.

"Party" was the wrong word, she decided later. It wasn't a party. It was an event. Conneaut Lake was the largest natural lake within an easy drive of Pittsburgh. In the summertime, it was alive with vacationing Pennsylvanians who enjoyed water sports and leisure time. Today, it seemed to Jessica that most of those same Pennsylvanians had ended up at this house.

Five minutes after her arrival she lost track of Alex. It wasn't that he left her. She had taken matters into her own hands immediately and made herself available to several young men who had eyed her appreciatively when she was introduced to them. She had been swept off to the water's edge where the food had been set under a striped canopy. Her plate had been heaped high, someone had drawn her a beer from an immense silver keg, and she had been installed on a lounge chair amid a circle of admirers.

Whatever she had learned about flirting at Oberlin seemed to be working with Alex's friends. They were impressed with her wit, and charmed by her smile. One young man, Grant Peters, a doctor from a nearby county, seemed especially fascinated. Jessica realized that although she had given him no more encouragement than she had given anyone else, his intentions had been made known to the others. Soon she was alone with him, and the conversation was turning serious.

"You came with Alex Grainger, didn't you?" Grant asked her.

Jessica examined the blond man with the serious blue eyes. "That's right."

"Have you known him long?"

"She certainly has." Alex seemed to step out of nowhere. "Move over, Jessie." Without a trace of formality Alex pushed her to the side of the lounge chair and dropped down beside her. He settled his arm around her shoulders.

Jessica tried to squirm out of his hold, but between his hip and the arm of the chair, she was stuck.

"Jessie and I go way back," Alex told Grant. "Way back."

"Well, I'm going to see if there's any more cake," Grant said. He leaped to his feet as if he couldn't get away fast enough. "Can I bring you anything?"

"Don't worry about us," Alex said. "I'll take care of Jessie."

"You're going to explain your behavior to me, aren't you?" Jessica asked after Grant left.

"Grant's got a terrible reputation."

"As bad as yours?"

"Well, not quite," Alex said with a trace of pride.

"Let me see if I have this straight. It's not all right for me to spend time with Grant Peters because he has a terrible reputation, but it is all right for me to be seen snuggling in this lounge chair with you even though your reputation is worse than his." Jessica had given up squirming in favor of relaxing against Alex. Now she turned slightly so that her soft curves were resting against the hard lines of his body.

"But you know me."

"I thought the point of this little outing was to introduce me to eligible young men."

"It is. Just not as eligible as Grant Peters."

"You're making no sense."

Alex didn't answer, as if he, too, realized the inherent paradox.

"Alex?"

"All right." He slid down to the bottom of the lounge and got to his feet. Jessica lectured her traitorous body. The feel of Alex brushing against her as he removed himself from her side had been too sensuous to ignore.

Grant kept his distance, but Jessica struck up a conversation with an attractive attorney who admitted to a secret fetish for redheads. They had settled on a blanket some distance from the group and were sharing histories when Alex joined them.

He wasted no time. "Did Jessica tell you that she's

just twenty-two?'' Alex asked. "She seems much older, doesn't she?''

The attorney was not put off so easily. "I've never thought age was that important.''

"That's right,'' Alex continued good-naturedly. "I'd forgotten. Your second wife was barely out of her teens.''

Jessica and the attorney had not gotten that far in their life stories, but Jessica was outraged that the damning information had come from Alex. "Don't you have someone you have to see?'' she asked him pointedly.

"Only you.'' He reached for her hand and held it, despite her attempts to shake him off. "After all, you're my date.''

The attorney seemed to know when he had been bested. "Nice talking to you, Jessica.'' He nodded to Alex and then he was gone.

"I am not your date.'' This time she succeeded in removing her hand from his. "Get off my blanket.''

Alex stroked his mustache and watched her. "I don't remember seeing you angry before. You were always such a docile little thing.''

"Get off my blanket. Now!''

"You're acting like a temperamental redhead.''

"And you're talking in stereotypes!'' Jessica stood. "All right. If you're not going to leave, I will.'' She flounced off to mingle with the crowd. Someone had set up huge speakers and turned on a stereo. There were gyrating bodies everywhere, and eventually, without Alex acting as guard dog at her side, she was invited to dance.

As a teenager Jessica had believed she had inher-

ited two left feet. As a college student she had realized that losing her shyness was the first key to becoming a good dancer. As soon as she quit worrying
about what she was doing, she had learned to do it
well. Now she allowed her feeling for the music to
express itself through her body, and dancing was a
pleasure.

She danced with first one man and then another.
There was such a tangled mass of people churning up
the grass that at times she wasn't sure who her partner
was.

Alex stayed away until she was on her third dance
with a young man whose name she hadn't even had
time to learn. It was a slow dance, and Jessica was
grateful for the rest. Two turns into it, however, her
partner changed.

"Your energy is boundless," Alex said, wrapping
his arms around her waist to pull her against him.

"Your gall is boundless. What was wrong this
time?"

"Your former partner's going through a messy di-
vorce right now. I wouldn't want you involved."

"We were dancing, not cohabiting!"

Alex pulled her a little closer, and Jessica was reminded of the endless dreams of her adolescence. Just
how many times had she wished that she and Alex
were drifting dreamily around a dance floor together?

One of Alex's hands traveled up her back, smoothing over the warm skin as it found its way to the nape
of her neck. In a moment he had unsnapped the clasp
around her ponytail and released her hair.

"Was that to cover me from view?" she asked.
The question was a little less sharp than she had in-

tended. She could still feel Alex's gentle touch on her skin.

"Be quiet and enjoy this dance."

She obeyed simply because there was absolutely nothing that she could think of to say. She was overcome with the sensation of Alex's thighs against hers, his hands on the bare skin of her waist.

When the music ended, Alex kept his hands in place as he stepped back. "I've got to get home now," he said. "Are you ready?"

She nodded, and then a faint smile tugged at her lips. "Actually I did have another offer for a ride home."

"Forget it."

They found their host to say goodbye, and in a few minutes they were on their way back to Lindleton. Now that Alex was no longer touching her, Jessica found that her tongue was working again. It was time for them to straighten out their relationship.

The sun had gone down, but the stars were not yet visible when she began.

"Look, Alex. I know you've known me most of your life, and that makes you feel protective. But I'm never going to go anywhere with you again unless you promise to cut out the 'I'm taking care of my sister' routine." Jessica kept her face straight ahead and her voice calm.

There was no answer from Alex's side of the car.

Jessica plunged on. "I realize you still think of me as a child, but I'm all grown up now. I can take care of myself."

"Can you?" Alex didn't sound sure that he believed her.

"I can," she reaffirmed. "Those were not the first men that I've been ogled by."

"What other firsts have come and gone, Jessica?"

Jessica couldn't believe that he had actually asked that question. No matter how protective he felt, he had no right to ask something so intensely personal. She was angry and hurt that he could be so insensitive. "That's absolutely none of your business." She surprised herself when her eyes filled with tears and she blinked them back, refusing to allow them to fall.

"You're right. I'm sorry."

Jessie turned her head just enough to see how hard his hands were gripping the steering wheel. Even in the twilight she could see how white his knuckles were. "You're a fine one to ask questions," she said, hurt pride in every word. "You're so proud of your reputation as the consummate lover. But not everyone falls into bed with anyone who's the least bit attractive. Just don't suspect me of behaving the way you do."

"I said I was sorry."

"But not enough to stay out of my life."

"I'm not used to feeling responsible for a woman. It's going to take some getting used to."

"I don't want you to feel responsible for me!"

"I can't just stop because you say so." The Porsche reacted to Alex's words with a sudden surge of speed.

Jessica was aware of barns and farmhouses and the clear gray silhouettes of trees against the deepening night sky. She sat back and watched the scenery, too upset to continue trying to make him understand her feelings. She had come to the party with the idea that seeing her with other men might provoke some form of jealousy from Alex. She had not expected this heavy dose of protectiveness. She was, after everything, nothing more than little Jessica Cassidy who needed to be taken care of. And although she wasn't sure what she did want from Alex, she knew that protection was what she didn't.

The car slowed as they neared Lindleton. They drove through the streets in silence, taking the road to the Bancrofts' house after they had passed through town. In the Bancrofts' driveway Alex turned off the engine and opened his door. Jessica was out of the car and walking through the trees toward the house before he could come around to help her.

"Jessie?"

If his voice had been demanding, she wouldn't have stopped for him. But Alex's voice was a soft question, and she couldn't resist him when he was gentle. She stopped. "What?" she asked without turning around.

His arms circled her waist, and he laid his cheek against her head. "I don't know what got into me tonight. I don't think of you as a little girl. I don't know what I think."

Jessica sighed as his hands stroked the soft, firm skin exposed by the halter top. "I find this confusing. One minute you want to introduce me to men, the next you do everything you can to keep me from getting to know the men you introduce me to, then you question me about my virginity like an old-fashioned papa."

"Turn around." Alex put his hands on her shoulders and spun her to face him. "I was out of line."

She nodded, ready, finally, to accept his apology. "All right."

He raised his hand to her face to brush a strand of hair off her cheek. His hand lingered, joined soon by his other one to frame her face. He smoothed his thumbs over her mouth as if reluctant to do more or to do less. And then with a sigh that was barely audible he bent and brushed her mouth with his.

Jessica understood the kiss for what it was. He was telling her that he was sorry, that he wouldn't succumb to his strange emotions again, that he hoped she understood.

But that was the first kiss. The second kiss had no explanation. He had drawn away as if to say goodnight, sighed once more as if he knew that he was making a mistake, and then bent to kiss her again.

At first she wasn't sure that a response was called for. All Alex's kisses had been casual and friendly and brief. There had been no time, no reason to respond. But this kiss was different. It began as gentle persuasion, but then it deepened quickly into a dark pleasure that penetrated her body as if he were kissing every part of her.

She wanted to hold back. His feelings weren't to be trusted; her feelings weren't to be trusted. But there seemed to be no way to keep herself apart from the kiss. She parted her lips before she realized it, and her hands went around his neck to tunnel in his hair. Alex pulled her closer, and she exploded with the pleasure of his body fully against her own. Even when they had danced together he had not held her this tightly.

If she had dreamed of Alex's kisses when she was

sixteen, she had not dreamed that they would destroy her will or her rationality. What did it matter that he had a string of women who, hand to hand, would reach over the seas to Australia? What did it matter that she was not experienced enough to deal with his kind of loving? And leaving.

Nothing seemed to matter. Nothing but the feel of his body against hers, his tongue stroking hers, his attention tearing her heart to tiny shreds.

"What am I doing?"

Jessica wasn't sure who had said the words, although she suspected that they had come from Alex. No matter. It could just as easily have been her. She stepped back and tried to catch her breath. She knew her eyes were wide with emotion.

"Jessie." He reached out to smooth her hair from her face, tangling his hands in it briefly as if that pleasure was too much to give up suddenly.

She wanted to say something clever. Something that would show him how sophisticated she was and how able to handle this kind of intimacy. Instead, she could only stare.

"Too much moon," Alex said finally. "Too much moon and too many shared memories."

How could memories of pigtail pulling and formal country club parties lead to this kind of kissing? And the moon? Well, the moon had gone behind clouds probably not to return until tomorrow.

"Good night, Alex." She was proud that she could say something. Jessica turned and followed the path to the house.

"Jessie?"

She stopped, without turning around.

"Sweet dreams."

She stood quietly until she heard his car drive away. As she opened the front door she wondered if he had any idea what kind of dreams she was certain to have that night.

Chapter Five

Although Molly Bancroft was shy and relatively undemanding, when she wanted something badly enough she could be as stubborn as her brother. On the Saturday following the Conneaut Lake party, Jessica was treated to an example of Molly's tenacity.

"And Alex is coming. You have to come, too, Jessica. It won't be any fun if you're not there!"

One of the things Jessica had learned to appreciate in the Bancroft household was spontaneity. The past week had been dreary and dull. This day, however, had dawned with a brilliant blue sky and a promise of golden sunshine for morning and afternoon. Not only was Ben home, but also there were no babies expected immediately. The occasion called for a trip to nearby Drake's Well, the site of the first productive oil well in the United States, to ride back and forth on the nine-mile bike trail and visit the park itself. The whole family was going. And by now, no one

thought of a family outing without automatically including Jessica.

Now Jessica cataloged the expressions on Molly's
face. The pretty teenager resembled a silent movie
heroine pleading for her life or the preservation of her
virtue. She was difficult to resist.

"I'm just not sure I'm up to such a long ride,"
Jessica said, hedging as best she could. "It's been a
long time since I was on a bike." She didn't add that
it had been exactly fourteen years. The bike had belonged to a friend, and Jessica hadn't ridden it. She
had perched on the high seat, lifting first one foot and
then the other to see how well she could balance.
Afterward she had asked her parents if she could have
a bike of her own so that she could learn to ride.
Overprotective to a fault, they had been horrified.

Molly wasn't ready to accept Jessica's excuses.
"But the bike path is only a slight grade and it's
downhill coming back. It's smooth and wide and you
don't have to worry about traffic. You'll love it."

"It's very nice of you to want me to come," Jessica began, wondering why she just didn't admit the
truth, "but I think I'm going to stay home and finish
a book I'm reading."

"What's the matter, Jessie? Are you worried about
a little fresh air?" Alex lounged in the doorway, one
elbow propped on the frame. Jessica wondered just
how long he'd been listening.

"Alex, make Jessica come, too," Molly wheedled.

"Just give us a few minutes alone. I'll persuade
her."

Smiling triumphantly, Molly left to finish getting
ready for the trip.

"Hello, Alex." Jessica faced the man she hadn't seen in a week. She decided to pretend that the kiss she had been trying to analyze ever since had never happened. "How have you been?"

"Busy. Lonely." The corners of his mouth lifted, and his eyes crinkled in a one-hundred-percent-Alex smile. "How about you?"

"Busy." She smiled, too. Her smile was basic Jessica. Polite, lovely and just a bit too serious.

"Why aren't you planning to come today?"

She had been the victim of Alex's teasing too many times to tell him the truth. She could feel herself being sucked into a morass of little white lies. "I just thought a quiet day might be nice."

"Is that it? Or were you reluctant to spend the day with me after last weekend?" Now his smile was seductive. Jessica had seen him use it on other women often enough. He had never used it on her, however. At least not to this degree. She was being treated to a full-scale attack.

"What am I supposed to be reluctant about?" she countered. It was silly, really, not to surrender. She had already lost this battle; unless she told him the truth, he wouldn't believe that she was refusing to go for any reason other than fear of him.

"Aren't you worried about losing control of yourself?"

She knew he was teasing. His ego was not that inflated. "I can handle *you*, if that's what you're really referring to," she said.

"Good—then you have no reason not to go. I can certainly handle you."

"You've never understood the word no."

"Please come, Jessie." He had turned serious, and both his eyes and his smile were softer. Pleading.

She had been prepared to dig in her heels and stand up to him. But, as always, she was no match for the gently persuasive Alex, only the egotistical, demanding one. Alex had always been able to get what he wanted from everyone.

"All right." What was she doing? She had just agreed to go on an eighteen-mile bike hike when she had never ridden a bike at all. She opened her mouth to call back her words, but the only thing to emerge was one last pitiful question. "Do they rent bicycles there?" With training wheels? she added silently.

"Nothing fancy. You'll probably have to do with a one-speed."

Jessica nodded, sending a plea to heaven that all the bicycles would be rented by the time they arrived. "I've got to go change."

What did she wear when she was deliberately setting out to make a fool of herself? Appropriate attire would be a helmet, knee and elbow pads and a pillow tied to her derriere. Lacking that, she chose a turquoise jogging suit over a short-sleeved ivory pullover. She took one last peek in the mirror to memorize what the premortified Jessica looked like, and went out to join the others.

Lydia and Molly had loaded backpacks full of sandwiches and soft drinks in cans for each of them. Jessica and Alex wrapped cookies and added fruit while the rest of the family finished dressing. Too soon they were ready for the short trip to Titusville where Drake's Well was located.

Clancy begged to ride in the Porsche with Alex and

Jessica, and there was no time for intimate conversation on the drive. Jessica was immensely grateful to Clancy. She spent the time trying to mentally teach herself to ride a bicycle. How hard could it be, after all? She was an adult. She had been walking for years. Obviously she could balance. She knew how to put one foot in front of the other; she knew how to steer. All she had to do was sit on the seat and ride down the road.

They parked their cars near the bike rental shop. Alex and Ben got the Bancroft bicycles off the station wagon roof rack that accommodated four bicycles, and then Alex turned to Jessica. "Do you mind if they start without us? We can catch up after we get our bikes."

"No problem," she said too quickly. Making a fool of herself in front of Alex was bad enough. Doing it in front of the whole Bancroft clan was unimaginable.

"We'll wait," Lydia and Molly said together.

"Please don't," Jessica said. Her voice was one degree away from a plea.

"Let them catch up later," Ben said, smiling slightly.

Jessica knew that Ben thought she wanted to be alone with Alex, but at this point she didn't care what anyone imagined about her motives.

"We'll ride slowly," Lydia promised, maneuvering her red three-speed across the parking lot and on to the road that led to the trail. "If you don't catch up, we'll meet you at Drake's Well."

At the bike rental shop Alex left Jessica outside to pick out a bike that suited her while he paid their fees. Jessica wanted to tell him that none of the bikes suited, the only thing that did suit her was curling up in the back of the Bancrofts' station wagon and sleeping while everyone else rode the trail. But the shreds of pride she still clung to kept her from telling him the truth.

The moment of reckoning arrived when Alex came out of the shop, pocketing his wallet. Jessica watched as he selected the largest bicycle available and draped his long-legged body over the seat. "Ready?"

"Alex, I haven't ridden a bike in a long time." Surely that wasn't too much of a lie. Forever was a long time. "It may take me a while to remember how. You go ahead. I'll catch up."

"I wouldn't consider leaving you. You'll be amazed how quickly it will come back to you." He pedaled out of the parking lot and Jessica followed behind, walking beside the bike and holding it stiffly away from her body as if it were a mad dog.

There were cars on the road leading to the trail. "I don't think I feel comfortable enough to ride in traffic," she yelled to Alex. "You go ahead to the trail. I'll catch up and get on my bike there."

Instead Alex swung himself off the seat while his bike was still in motion and turned it around to wait for her. Jessica could almost see the truth dawn as she watched the changing expressions on his face.

"Jessie," he said softly, "there were only two cars and they turned off at the parking lot."

"You can't be too careful."

"Lord, I hear your mother's voice."

"That's not funny, Alex!"

"It wasn't meant to be funny." Alex waited until she was beside him before he continued. "The way

Marion and Robert protected you used to worry my father and mother. Especially my father. Most of the time he was sure he had done the right thing to place you with them, but sometimes, when he saw the price you paid for having a mother and father so much older..."

"That's enough!"

He ignored her. "They wouldn't let you ride a bike, would they?"

At least she hadn't had to tell him the truth herself. "No, and I never learned to skate or ski, either. I didn't drive a car until I was a junior in college, and I've never been any closer to a horse than a merry-go-round. And even then my mother stood beside me." She lifted her chin. "Now you know."

He listened with his head cocked slightly. When she finished his eyes were warm. "I'm a lucky man. I can't believe there are so many wonderful things left to teach you."

She almost dropped her bicycle. She had expected him to tease her or worse, to pity her. She had not expected this genuine pleasure at the prospect of helping her learn about all the things she had missed. A flood of affection washed through her body. She wasn't sure what else was between them, but one thing was certain. Alex cared about her, and he wouldn't let her down.

"So," he continued, "it's time for your first lesson. Follow me." He turned and began to walk his bike to the beginning of the bike path. Jessica followed behind.

"I'm sorry I yelled at you," she apologized when they reached the trail. Clancy had informed Jessica in the car that the bike trail was actually an old railroad track that had been paved over. It followed the path of Oil Creek, a tributary of the Allegheny River, and it meandered along like the most unchallenging of country lanes. Jessica had expected something more difficult than this wide, smooth expanse. Her fear of failure eased a little.

"I didn't mean to criticize your parents," Alex said. "I just wanted you to know that I understood."

"Thank you."

"And now we're going to ride the trail together."

Before she could protest his confidence, he began his instruction. "Teaching Jessica to ride a bike. Lesson One. First you have to get the feel of it under you. Swing your leg over the seat. That's right. Jessie, that bike's too short for you."

"I like the idea of being close to the ground."

"You're not going to like it by the time we get to the end of the trail. Your leg can't extend properly and you'll end up with cramps."

Cramps seemed like a small price to pay for the comfort of terra firma so close to her toes. "What's next?"

"Lesson Two. Put your feet on the pedals. When you feel yourself teetering, put your feet on the ground." Alex demonstrated with his bicycle.

Jessica tried, amazed that an adult who could sit perfectly still anytime she wanted was incapable of maintaining her balance on this seemingly sturdy piece of machinery.

"Do you see how difficult it is?"

She nodded, both feet firmly on the ground again.

"Well, it's much easier when you're moving.

That's the good news. The bad news is that now we have to get you moving.''

"That is bad news."

Alex pushed his own bike to the side of the trail, leaning it against a small embankment. "Anyone who can coordinate her fingers on a piano keyboard can ride a bicycle. I'm going to push you so you can get the feel of balancing and pedaling at the same time. I won't let you fall."

"I think I'd rather try on my own. Al-l-ex!"

"Just hold on and steer, Jessie. That's what the handlebars are for."

"How do I stop this thing?"

"I'll tell you when you need to know. Otherwise you'll be stopping it all the time." Although they were beginning to gather speed, the exertion hardly showed on Alex as he ran beside her.

In spite of herself, Jessica found that balancing and pedaling were not as difficult as they had first seemed. She concentrated on keeping the bicycle on the path. Obviously Alex couldn't do it all by himself. They weren't going fast enough for her to feel the wind rushing through her hair or the marvelous sensation of flying freedom, but she could begin to imagine what it would be like. She was suddenly the eight-year-old Jessica who wanted desperately to be free of the confines of her sheltered life.

Without thinking about it, she began to pedal harder. It was an amazing phenomenon, this ability to balance better the faster you went. She laughed out loud at the experience. By now she knew she was doing a lot of the work herself. Alex had slipped behind to push the back of the bicycle. Jessica experienced the heady sensation of keeping her own balance. Surely Alex couldn't be helping much from the rear.

"This is great," she said with confidence. "Take your hands off for a minute and let me see if I can do it by myself."

There was no answer, which seemed strange, but Jessica assumed Alex was too winded by now to talk. Nothing seemed different, and she wondered if he had heard her. "I said take your hands off."

When there was still no change, she hazarded a backward glance. Alex was bending down, at the beginning of the trail, retrieving his own bicycle. She would never know if the shock of finding that she had been pedaling alone for what looked like a city block, or the attempt to see behind her caused her downfall, but before she could make sense of her situation, Jessica found herself sprawled in the middle of the bike path, a tangle of metal spokes and arms and legs.

"Are you all right?" Alex leaped from his bicycle to pull her from the wreckage.

Jessica moaned and kept her eyes firmly closed until Alex had removed the bicycle from on top of her. When he leaned over to examine her, she waited until he was squatting precariously before she sprang to a sitting position and began to tickle him.

"You rat! You left me!"

Relieved, Alex grabbed her hands, but not before he had been knocked off balance by her assault. Jessica sprawled on top of him, fighting to retrieve her hands so that she could continue.

"Is this the serious Miss Jessica Cassidy?" Alex was laughing in spite of himself, trying to simulta-

neously sit up and keep her hands imprisoned in his
own. "We're going to be run down by the next bikers
to come down the trail," he warned as she continued
to fight him.

"I'll leap off you at the last minute and leave you
to their mercy," she promised between giggles.

"I won't allow it." Steadily, Alex pulled her down
to his chest with Jessica fighting all the way. "You
realize how foolish we look, don't you?"

"I hope one of your patients sees us."

"What a nasty tongue you have, woman." Before
Jessica realized his intention, Alex had pulled her
firmly on top of him and his mouth had silenced any
more of her insults. He kissed her firmly, accepting
no resistance. Then he was rolling to the side to de-
posit her on the trail before he got to his feet and
pulled her to stand beside him.

"You just can't be trusted, can you?" Jessica said,
keeping her voice light. Neither of them was sure
whether she referred to the riding lesson or the kiss.

Alex began to brush the dust from the road off her
jogging suit. He took a comb from his pocket and,
despite her protests, he pulled it through her hair, demanding that she stand still while he finished. Despite
the humor in his voice the act was intimate and plea-
surable. Jessica allowed him to continue.

It was her turn next to brush the dust and little
pieces of gravel off his jeans, consciously avoiding
any area he might consider provocative. She dusted
off his blue shirt, too, stopping at the top button and
impishly unbuttoning one, then two buttons to reveal
a little more of his chest. "You'll get too hot," she

explained carefully, but she knew the color in her cheeks had deepened as she said the words.

"What am I going to do with you?"

Since it was the question she was asking herself, she had no answer. She avoided his eyes, turning back to examine her bike. "It doesn't look any worse for wear."

"You didn't get scraped up, did you?"

She shook her head, her back still turned. "I'm fine. I caught myself before I fell. Everything just sort of crumpled at the last second."

"Then it's time for Lesson Three. Relaxing and enjoying what you've learned." Alex mounted his own bicycle. "Ready?"

She wasn't, but she wasn't going to admit it. This was no time to quit. Reluctantly she got back on the bike. "Ready."

It took a long series of wobbles and a near fall to get moving fast enough so that she could balance herself with relative ease. Wisely, Alex said nothing, riding slowly beside her, but still far enough away not to give her a target to crash into.

Jessica was just beginning to enjoy herself when she saw what looked like a mountain ahead of her. "Holy Cow!"

"Just pedal as hard as you can. It's only a little hill," Alex said calmly. "You're doing great. I've never seen anyone do better." He kept up the steady stream of compliments as she struggled to propel the bike up the hill. It was Mount Kilimanjaro, Mount Everest, Mount Impossible all rolled into one, and Jessica was sure that it had been plopped down in the middle of the bike path during the past five minutes just to test her. Obviously if it had been there all the time, no one would ever want to ride the trail in the first place.

At the top, she dragged her feet on the ground to stop so that she could rest.

"That was magnificent," Alex assured her. "Now comes the fun part. Just watch me, and when you come down, remember to concentrate on steering. The bike will do the rest. By the way, that was the only hill. You're home free from here."

He sailed down the hill with a whoosh, and Jessica watched from the top. His delighted laughter seemed to hover in the air behind him. "Your turn," he called.

How difficult could it be? She had done the hard part. This was the reward, wasn't it? Recklessly she pushed off. It wasn't until she was a quarter of the way down that she realized Alex never had told her how to stop the bicycle. She was flying free, all right; she was gathering speed with each inch, and she had no idea how she was to control it. She only knew that if she dragged her feet at this velocity she'd topple over like a cornstalk at harvest.

"Al-l-l-l-ex! How do I stop this thing?"

"Peddle backward. Not too suddenly. Jessie!"

She was lurching over the road, fighting the machine beneath her that seemed suddenly to have gone berserk. Gravity was more powerful than she was, and she was still heading down, but not in the straight line in which she had begun. A little knowledge was a dangerous thing. Hitting the brakes with all her power had not been a good idea.

She might have succeeded, anyway, except for one

small pothole in the otherwise smoothly paved road. Perhaps if she'd been in control she could have avoided it, but struggling to stay upright had taken all her effort. When she realized she was going to hit the pothole, she shut her eyes and prayed.

This time when she moaned, it was not an act.

"Jessie? Are you all right?"

At least she had ended up on the soft shoulder of the bike path. She opened her eyes and hoped that only one Alex would appear. She was in luck. "Would you check and see if I left any body parts on the trail?" she asked politely.

He heaved the bicycle away from her and cradled her against him. "Poor baby. Are you all right? Are you hurt?"

"Aren't you supposed to leave me undisturbed until an ambulance gets here?"

He kissed her forehead and examined her face. "All right so far." He began to run his hands down her arms. "Does anything hurt?"

"My pride and my bottom. And one knee is scraped."

"I'm not sure I can do anything about the first two, but let me check the third." He positioned her on his lap so that he could roll up her pants leg. "It's going to be a nasty bruise tomorrow," he warned her. "We'll have to see if you can stand on it." He pulled her back against him. "You're going to want a new teacher now, aren't you?"

She lay back in his arms and thought that there was nothing she didn't want Alex to teach her. Absolutely nothing. She had turned to lean against him, and she could feel her soft breasts push against his chest. Even now, with the casualness of his embrace, she could feel her body respond to him. It wasn't the response of a teenager with a crush. It was the response of a woman, hungry and willing. She moved slightly to defuse her own reaction. "You can be so nice sometimes," she said, resting her head against his shoulder. "I think I'll keep you."

His arms tightened around her, and she felt him kiss her hair. When he finally loosened his grip, she stood up, glad to be released from the temptation of his touch. Gingerly she tested her knee. It bore her weight with no trouble, and she flexed it several times, satisfied that it wasn't too sore. Alex stood, too.

"We'll go back. We can walk to the parking lot and then drive over to the park to tell Ben and Lydia that you had an accident. We'll have our picnic there."

"Not on your life. My bike wasn't damaged, was it?" Jessica began to brush off her jogging suit. This time instead of gravel she removed sticks and leaves and powdery black soil.

"No."

"Then let's go."

"Are you sure?"

She smiled. "Absolutely. Look, I've learned to pedal and balance, I've learned to start and stop, and I've learned how to go up and how *not* to go down a hill. I've got it all mastered. Now comes the fun."

"You may be sore tomorrow," he warned. "You probably shouldn't push it."

She stood on her tiptoes and kissed the worry lines on his forehead. "Aren't you nice to be so concerned?" she asked in a husky voice.

He stood quietly when she had moved away and watched her mount the bicycle yet again. It was only when he saw that she was absolutely serious about continuing that he got on his own and followed behind her.

Someone had thoughtfully marked the miles of the trail. Each time they passed one, Jessica shouted with elation. After four miles without another accident, Alex insisted that they stop and rest. They turned into a small clearing that had been furnished with picnic tables and parked their bikes next to one. Jessica had never appreciated the luxury of stretching her legs to their full capacity as much as she did at that moment. Nor had she appreciated the luxury of a bench that accommodated her entire bottom.

"Tell me if I'm way out of line," Alex said as he pulled grapes out of his backpack to share with her. "But are you finally having fun?"

Fun? The word seemed inadequate to label the emotion she was feeling. She wasn't having fun. She had reached a state of almost pure euphoria. The warm sun on her skin, the breeze ruffling her hair, the proud old trees and the rippling creek that appeared now and then beside the trail had joined in a conspiracy to make her feel freer and happier than she remembered having felt in a long time. "I love it," she told Alex, unable to describe her emotions any other way.

"You feel things right down to your toes, don't you? I never realized it before."

She was surprised at his question. Had he thought that the serious Miss Jessica Cassidy was the real woman? The only woman? She nodded, uncertain whether his realization of how emotional she really was would be a blessing or a curse. "What about you, Alex? Does a day like this make you sing inside?"

"Being with you seems to have that effect on me."

She waited for his eyes to crinkle in humor or for his lips to raise in his most seductive of smiles. Neither happened. He seemed to be as startled as she was at his answer. She popped a grape in her mouth to cover up the silence.

When they had finished, Alex took her hand and they wandered through the woods investigating gnarled roots and low-hanging birds' nests. Since Jessica had never thought of Alex as anything but a city man, she was delighted to find that he had a love for nature that made him spend as much time outdoors as he could.

"I'm an avid cross-country skier," he told her. "I think you'd love it, too."

"I'm sure I would." She imagined Alex teaching her with the same patience and concern he had shown as he taught her to ride her bike. Of course, if he ever did teach her, she'd find out how to stop before she even pulled on a ski boot. "I've always loved winter, but I hate staying indoors so much of the time. Skiing would solve that."

"There are cross-country trails in Pittsburgh."

But Alex wouldn't be there. "I'm sure you're right." She hesitated before adding, "But I'm not sure that's where I'll settle."

"Oh?"

"I just haven't made any decisions yet."

"That sounds wise." He slipped his arm around her waist to guide her back to their bicycles. "You've got plenty of time to decide about life plans. You've got the whole world out there to choose from.''

Somehow, having the whole world available didn't sound appealing, but she agreed politely.

At their bicycles, Alex examined her knee once again to be sure it wasn't swelling. Jessica marveled at the way her leg could feel with his hands running up and down its smooth curves. She wanted to ask him to examine the other one, but she didn't.

The next four miles flew by quickly, although Jessica could feel them taking their toll. When the trail ended, passing over a bridge and into traffic before they turned off at the Drake Well Memorial Park, she was confident in her ability to face the new obstacles and glad that she was soon going to be able to take an extended rest.

They pulled their bikes into the parking lot, and Alex produced a lock Clancy had given him so that they could leave them safely.

''Here they are!'' Molly stood and waved, and Jessica and Alex joined the Bancrofts on a blanket by the creek. There would be plenty of time later to see the exhibits and the small well that still pumped up a residue of oil. Now all she could do was sit and groan.

''Poor tired Jessica,'' Alex sympathized.

''Did you run over her a few times?'' Lydia asked Alex, her voice stern. ''Jessica looks beat.''

''Beat up,'' Clancy said helpfully.

''I hit a pothole,'' Jessica explained before Alex could tell her secret. ''Alex had to pick me up off the ground and put me back together.''

''And here we thought you were leisurely enjoying each other's company,'' Ben teased them both.

Jessica looked up to smile at him and saw the distress on Lydia's face as she turned. It wasn't disapproval. It was concern. Concern way beyond the bounds of friendship. She realized that Lydia was as worried about her relationship with Alex as she was about Molly's relationship with Mike. There was no reason to feel that she owed Lydia reassurance, but Jessica heard herself giving it, anyway.

"There was nothing leisurely about that trip," she said casually. "But I did enjoy it even if I had to work to keep up with Alex the whole way."

Alex, too, seemed to need to give reassurance. "On the way back," he said with a smile, "I'll take Clancy as my biking partner. Now there's a friend who knows how to ride."

It was a simple exchange, but as Jessica caught Alex's eye, she understood his message. Whatever is between us, he told her with his expression, we will not burden Lydia with it. Jessica agreed silently that she, too, would not give the older woman unnecessary cause for concern. Whatever Lydia's reasons for her fears, they were very real to her, and Jessica cared too much to worry her.

Chapter Six

"There's not a part of me that feels that it wants to be attached to this body." Jessica was standing stiffly at the piano. Molly was seated beside her on the bench.

"You look like you'll fall apart if somebody sneezes in your direction." Molly giggled, and then she clapped her hand over her mouth as if she were afraid she'd hurt Jessica's feelings.

"Go ahead. Laugh at me." Jessica tried to stand straighter and raise her chin in the air, but even that effort at mock dignity was too painful. She groaned.

"You haven't been off your feet all day."

"I'm afraid if I deviate from this position I'll faint from the agony."

Molly giggled again, and Jessica managed a smile to show her she was forgiven.

"I guess the whole bike trail yesterday was too much for a beginner," Molly said when she was able to be serious again.

"What makes you think I was a beginner?"

"I rode back with you, remember? I've never seen so many wobbles in my life."

"That obvious, huh?"

"You're paying for your sins, Jessica. 'Pride goeth before a fall,'" Molly said righteously.

"A lot of help you are. Here I expected sympathy and I get a lecture. Let's hear your D Major scale in triplets, three octaves."

Jessica bent over to correct Molly's hand position and groaned again.

"One, two, three..." Molly counted. "One, two, three... Jess-i-ca... why-don't-you... let-me-take ... care-of-your... prob-ba-lem?" she asked in time to the triplets. "I-know-a... way-you-can... make-it-feel...be-et-ter."

Jessica waited until Molly had completed the scale. "How? I'll do anything."

"Leave it to me. Trust me."

"Why do I feel like I'm getting a pitch from a used car salesman?"

Lydia opened the music room door and stepped in. "How's it going?"

"Fine." Jessica took a good look at Lydia and gave a low "Wow" of approval. "Don't you look beautiful."

"Thank you." Lydia twirled slowly to show off the brown-and-gold paisley dress.

"Yeah, Mom. Is that new?"

"It is. Your father is taking me to dinner tonight. I wanted to see if you thought this would do."

"More than do," Molly said.

"Good. There's cold chicken in the refrigerator

from last night or frozen pizza in the big freezer downstairs if you'd rather have that. I made a salad to go with either.''

"Don't worry about us," Jessica assured her.

Lydia smiled a thank-you. "I'm going to meet Ben at the hospital in a little while. I'll see you both when I come home.''

"Well, that makes my plan easier," Molly said after her mother left.

"How?''

"You'll see.''

An hour later Jessica had managed to lower herself to the sofa and was lying down, feet propped on pillows, when Alex walked into the living room.

"I hear a doctor's needed.''

Jessica groaned and turned her face to the sofa cushions. Now she understood Molly's reluctance to explain her remedy for Jessica's aches and pains. "Go away. This is your fault.''

"How can you possibly say that? Who kept her sheltered past a secret until it was too late for me to help?''

Jessica refused to look at him but she knew he was grinning. "Go away and leave me to suffer in peace.''

"I've come to make it better.''

"Time will make it better.''

"My hot tub will make it better.''

She opened her mouth to refuse, but her imagination took flight instead. She could almost feel the warm water soaking away the soreness that permeated every muscle. She had tried the bathtub, but it was impossible to stretch out and let the water cover all of her. The hot tub would be perfect.

"I don't know..." Her response was embarrassingly transparent. Convince me, it said. Make me go against my better judgment.

"Turn around, Jessie."

She obliged with tremendous effort. There he was, Alex Grainger, the same wonderful hunk who had lived unchallenged in her daydreams for years unending, the same outrageously attractive man who couldn't seem to decide if she was still a pesky kid sister or a woman he desired. She wondered what decision the night would bring, because she knew that no matter what the consequences, she was going to go.

"Come home with me." He held out his hand.

She took it and Alex pulled her to a sitting position. She didn't even notice the pain because she was so busy trying to figure out why she was such an idiot.

"Molly says that Lydia is gone for the evening," he said.

"That's right."

"Then this will be easier."

She thought about his words as she slowly climbed the stairs to get her bathing suit and robe. So she had not imagined Alex's nonverbal acknowledgment of Lydia's concern about their relationship when they were at Drake's Well. Jessica had been curious from the beginning about Lydia's overprotectiveness with Molly. Now that it seemed to include her, she wanted some answers.

They were in the Porsche speeding toward the north of town before she had a chance to question

Alex. He had thoughtfully provided her with a small pillow from the Bancrofts' sofa, and she was perched higher than usual on the seat, trying to be sophisticated despite her sore bottom.

"I'd like to know what's going on with Lydia." She assumed Alex would understand to what she was referring.

"What do you mean?"

Jessica wondered why he sounded so startled. "Am I imagining it, or has Lydia put our relationship on the same level as Molly and Mike's?"

Alex was quiet as he turned off Lindleton's main street and began to wind along a more rural route. "You're not imagining it," he said finally. His voice sounded strangely relieved. Jessica wondered what question he had thought she was going to ask.

"I can understand...no, I can't understand, but I can accept the way she treats Molly. Why she's becoming so protective of me is the mystery."

Alex shook his head. "Not so much of one. Lydia cares about you. I think that having you live with them for the summer has made her regard you—" he paused and glanced at Jessica "—almost like a daughter. Whatever her reasons, she's worried about you just as she's worried about Molly."

"Why do you think she's that way?" His explanation made sense to Jessica, but she wanted to know more.

"I think that when Lydia was much younger she probably had a traumatic experience with a man. She doesn't want Molly or you to go through anything similar."

"But it doesn't make sense to try so hard to shield Molly, or me, either. We have to make mistakes."

"Sometimes people aren't sensible, Jessie. This is one of those times. Ordinarily Lydia's a perfectly rational human being. But a perceived threat to her children—" he paused again "—or to anyone she regards as highly as she regards you, makes her irrational."

"I know how much you like Lydia and Ben, but yesterday I got the feeling that you'd stop seeing me if you thought it would make Lydia feel better." Jessica realized that she had just confirmed that something was developing between them that might give Lydia cause to be upset. She didn't care. It was more important to have everything out in the open.

"I'm very fond of the Bancrofts. I'd do almost anything for either of them. But as you see, I'm sitting here and you're sitting there and we're going to my house. I'm glad we didn't have to flaunt it in Lydia's face, but I'd have come to get you, anyway."

"What changed your mind? Yesterday you rode off and left me in a cloud of dust rather than worry her."

Alex turned his head to let his eyes flicker quickly over her. The look was as potent as a caress. Jessica shivered from its power. "The same thing that evidently changed yours," he said. "Neither of us wants to hurt Lydia, but neither one of us is willing to step back in time and be what we once were to each other."

"Little Jessica and Big Brother Alex?"

He nodded. "But it would be easier that way, wouldn't it?"

Yes, it would be easier, she thought as they pulled into the long driveway that led to Alex's house. It

would be easier if she still regarded Alex as an unattainable hero. It would be easier if he thought of
her as a sister to protect or to ignore. But she'd never
believed that easier was best.

"What do you think?" Alex asked when they were
parked in front of his house.

"I can't wait to see the inside. But Alex, a barn?"

"You'll love it."

"I already do."

There was no mistaking the original purpose of the
building in front of them. It was several stories high
and absolutely square, with none of the jutting additions of a house. There were twin towers, which had
originally been used for ventilation, on the sloped
roof. Now they added the only touch of whimsy. It
was not a large barn; no silo had ever stored a winter's grain for voracious livestock, and no herd of
cows had waited inside to supply Lindleton with fresh
milk and cream. It had obviously been used to house
the animals and farm implements needed to provide
for one family's needs.

Alex had chosen to retain the barn's character when
he had decided to have it remodeled. The building
was still painted a traditional dark red; the double
doors leading inside were still sturdy and crisscrossed
with additional boards for strength. They weren't the
original doors, however, not unless a fine craftsman
had constructed them. Who would have wasted such
beautiful wood and such exquisite workmanship on
doors that were seen almost exclusively by cattle and
an occasional mule?

"You must live upstairs." Jessica had noticed that
windows graced what must surely be the second story

now. They were placed symmetrically and in keeping
with the simplicity of the building's lines. She suspected that they had been added when Alex remodeled.

"Come see." Alex unlocked the double doors and
slid them open. Jessica realized that they led to a garage. She waited as he parked the Porsche inside, and
then followed him in.

"Convenient," she pronounced.

"Very," he agreed.

The garage was ample for three or more cars. Alex
obviously used the extra space for storage. Jessica
noticed shelves with neatly labeled boxes, and on one
wall, she saw several pairs of cross-country skis hanging neatly beside a toboggan.

Alex unlocked the door leading from the garage
into the rest of the building and stood aside for her
to enter. She had expected more storage, but instead
she discovered a multipurpose room that covered the
rest of the first floor. It was huge, divided into areas
by groups of furniture and planters built of the same
light wood that paneled the room. The biggest surprise, however, was the windows. The front of the
house hadn't revealed the secrets of the sides and
back. Light poured in, giving the room a golden glow
even though the sun was now low on the horizon.

"It's beautiful. All these windows!"

"We don't get our fair share of the sun up here,
so I decided to make sure I could make use of every
bit we do get. It meant changing the character of the
building, but that seemed better than tearing it
down."

"Much better." Jessica wandered, examining each

portion of the room. A lush curry-colored carpet covered the floor, and Alex had picked up the same color in many of his furnishings. There were plants everywhere, making use of the pervasive light, and bright panels of hand-printed fabric that would have dwarfed any other room. On the west side of the house, Alex had added a brick fireplace with a massive hearth that wrapped all the way around it. On the east side in the far corner was a sunken hot tub. "You realize how decadent this is, don't you?"

"That was the whole point." Alex came up behind Jessica and put his arms around her waist. "I had a reputation to live up to."

"I'm sure this cinched it."

The hot tub was surrounded on two sides by glass doors leading out to a wooden deck. Jessica imagined that in the summer Alex slid the doors open to give the feel of being outside. In the winter he could sit in his tub and look out over the snowy landscape without freezing to death. The best of everything.

"Have you ever been in a hot tub?" Alex asked, tightening his arms around her.

"Once."

"That's too bad. I was hoping it was another one of those firsts I could help you with."

"Well, it will be the first time I've been in one with you." Jessica covered his hands with hers and leaned against him. There were no more illusions between them, it seemed. They had stopped pretending that her visit was therapeutic. In fact, Jessica had to admit to herself that she had hardly noticed a sore muscle since she had gotten out of the car.

"Did you have supper?" he asked, his voice very close to her ear.

She wanted to concentrate on the erotic feel of his warm breath on her earlobe. The question seemed irrelevant in comparison. She sighed a little and snuggled against him. "No."

She could feel his lips nuzzling her now, playing gently with the skin on the side of her cheek. "I haven't, either. I'll get cheese and crackers. We can eat later."

Jessica knew if she turned around now that Alex would kiss her. She knew the kiss could lead almost anywhere, and she knew that she wanted it to go further than it should. Before she could decide what to do, Alex had stepped away from her. "Come see the upstairs. This is my fun room, but that's where I live. You can change up there."

The second story had been divided into smaller rooms and was much more traditional than the downstairs. Wide hardwood planks on the floor were covered with brightly hued area rugs, and Alex had chosen comfortable upholstered furniture for the living room and for a small den. His bedroom had also been designed with an eye to comfort.

"You can change in here." Alex ushered her into his room and stood back to watch the expression on her face.

"I'm surprised you can make yourself leave in the morning." Jessica said the words with just the right amount of cynicism. She was proud that she had managed to say anything. For a moment she had been speechless.

Alex's bedroom clearly belonged to a bachelor who

used it for more than sleeping. In the center of the room was a bed that had to have been custom-made. Lindleton's furniture store would never have dared to stock something so gigantic. Where would they have put the rest of their inventory? Jessica, who had never considered herself a prude, was sure that the bed had been designed for an orgy. Or a harem.

"Where's the strobe light? The bedside bar? The overhead mirrors?" She walked around the bed and examined the rest of the room, which seemed tame in comparison.

"The bed's a joke. It was put together by some of my fellow residents as a present when I bought into my practice. It's actually four single beds connected by…" Alex evidently read the skepticism on Jessica's face. "You don't believe me, do you?" he asked with a grin.

"Where or how you sleep is your concern."

"How about with whom I sleep? Is that solely my concern, too?"

Jessica sat gingerly on the edge of the massive bed and began to take off her shoes. She ignored his question. "Is it safe to change in here? I won't appear next month in some sleazy theater as the star of *Jessica Disrobes*, will I?"

"My X-rated video equipment is in the shop for repairs."

Jessica thought that her good sense had obviously gone somewhere for repairs, too. What was she doing here? She was way out of her league.

"I should leave," Alex said, leaning against the doorframe and not looking as if he planned to move an inch.

"Only if you want me to undress. Otherwise you can stand there and we can chat. I'm comfortable."

"I'll get the cheese and meet you downstairs."

"Aren't you going to get your suit?"

"In my own house?" He held up his hands to stave off her protest. "It's downstairs. I'll see you in a few minutes."

Jessica continued to sit on the edge of the bed without moving after he'd disappeared. Just how many women had shared this monstrosity with Alex? She wondered if she could even count high enough to get close to the number. And why did it bother her? She had always known that Alex was on the prowl. It was part of his charm. He changed lovers as often as some people changed their sheets. He was the archetypal young man sowing his wild oats.

But why hadn't any of those oats rooted and flourished? Alex fell in love regularly. He fell out of love just as regularly. Jessica imagined that there were women all over Pennsylvania who had felt the whirlwind force of his attentions and were still wondering just what had hit them. He was an honest man, a man not without principles. Jessica was sure that he made no promises, that, in fact, he chose women who would not cling when he left them. But why hadn't he been caught by his own antics? Why, in the midst of one of his love affairs, hadn't he awakened to the dawning of real love, to the need for commitment?

She stood and began to pull her tan polo shirt over her head. When she had undressed she went to stand in front of the full-length mirror on the back of his bedroom door. Could Alex fall in love with this woman? Certainly she was not like the others. She lacked the sophistication to write off an affair. She was younger, less sure of her own attractions. She had been in love with him years before, and she was falling in love with him again. She was taking a terrible risk if she thought she could convince Alex to fall in love with her.

"Too bad, Jessica," she murmured to the innocent young woman in the mirror, "you haven't set foot in the hot tub and you're already in over your head."

Alex was sitting blissfully in the water when Jessica finally came downstairs. She had schooled herself not to clutch the terry-cloth robe around her body; she would not try to protect herself from his gaze. After all, the green bikini covered everything that society demanded she cover. And Alex was a doctor. He had seen more uncovered bodies than Hugh Hefner.

"I thought you'd fallen asleep," he said lazily.

"I'm not moving as fast as usual."

"Good."

She winced at his not-so-hidden meaning. "How's the water?"

"Perfect."

With studied nonchalance, Jessica began to untie her robe. "I hope this helps my poor aching body." She slipped off the robe and folded it, taking a barrette out of the pocket at the last minute to pin her hair on top of her head. She managed it all without looking at Alex one time.

"Lord, Jessie. When you decided to grow up, you didn't fool around."

She couldn't avoid his eyes any longer. They were

filled with enough male approval to keep her ego inflated for the rest of her life. "I'm not the type to fool around, Alex."

"That's a waste of nature's gifts."

Jessica lowered herself to the side of the tub and tested the water with her foot. "One degree hotter and you could cook a lobster in here."

"The hotter it is, the more relaxing. At a certain point you hardly even want to move."

"Is it at that point?"

Alex nodded.

"Good. I think I like you sluggish." She took a piece of cheese from a tray near the edge and ate it while Alex watched her. Then she slipped into the water and sighed as the heat began to penetrate her sore muscles. "You were right—this is just what I needed." She settled on the side of the tub away from Alex and reached for another piece of cheese.

"Why are you so far away?"

She nibbled thoughtfully. "You know the old saying about safety in numbers? Well, I've never believed it."

"Surely you can trust me." He treated her to a wolfish grin. "This is Alex, old friend, pseudo big brother, family physician."

"And this is Jessica, who understands you every bit as well as your own mother." She finished her cheese and convinced herself to swallow. Suddenly her throat felt as if it were closing.

Alex began to slide around the seat. "And what is it that you understand?"

"I understand that as good a doctor as you probably are, your healing instincts don't extend to Sun-

day evenings in a hot tub.'' Jessica shut her eyes and
sank lower in the water.

Alex's voice was close to her ear. ''Then why did
you choose a green bikini just like the one the lifeguard at the country club pool always wore?''

''That was before I saw your bed.''

His laugh was husky. ''And what does my bed
have to do with it?''

''You mean business, don't you, Alex?'' She
opened her eyes and found that he was almost on top
of her. ''Simple flirtations are not your style.''

''Are they your style?''

''Until now.''

She was ready when he kissed her. Her arms found
their way around his neck and she let the kiss take
them both where it would. Their other kisses had been
preliminary. This one was a kiss to build on.

His hands were framing her face, adjusting the
level and the angle of her mouth so that he could have
the access he seemed to crave. His mouth was as
warm as the water surrounding them and as deli-
ciously liquid. It moved over hers like a wave crashing into a yielding shoreline. She had no desire to
protest its intimacy.

Jessica twined her arms around him to anchor herself. She was floating with the rippling movements of
the water and with the pleasure rippling through her
body. Despite her cautious words, there was no part
of her that wanted to be rational, no part of her that
wanted to pull back. When his hands began to smooth
over her shoulders and make demands on her willing
flesh, she could only sigh her acceptance.

Alex pulled her against him, making short work of

the ribbon that tied the top of her bikini. When she could feel her bare breasts against his chest she moaned with pleasure, threading her fingers through his hair to pull his mouth to hers again. His hands were gentle, as if he knew that he was exploring uncharted territory, but he left no part of her untouched, stroking her softly and building her pleasure until she was as filled with heat as the water surrounding them.

Somehow she had known just what it would be like with him. She had known that he would understand her needs and that he would give her just the right amount of reassurance as he made his own demands on her. He whispered endearments as he took down her hair and filled his hands with it, letting it float like flame on the swirling water. He waited patiently for all the tension to leave her before he let his lips follow the path of his hands over her body, lifting her so that she was exposed to his gaze and to the sweet ministrations of his tongue.

"Where have you been all my life?" he asked before he gently took her into his mouth.

Jessica cried out from the sweetness of his caress, knowing as she did that she had exposed herself completely. Where had she been? She had been waiting for him to notice her. She had never stopped waiting, even during the years when she had hardly thought of him at all. She had kept a part of herself inviolate, hoping that someday she could give it to Alex Grainger.

"I had no idea that touching you would be this perfect." He held her tightly and let her slip by slow inches down his body. Standing so close, she could not fail to understand that he, too, was at the point of no return. "I had no idea that just holding you would be so hard."

"And that's all you intended? To hold me?" She heard the vulnerability in her words.

"I don't know what I intended. I think I've been fooling myself." His mouth pressed firmly against hers as if to block out his own thoughts.

Jessica moved against him opening to the kiss that threatened to drown them both in emotion. She felt Alex lift her again and she wrapped her legs around his hips. She realized that it would take very little for them to be even closer.

"Do you want this to be one of your firsts with me, Jessie? Surely you know that's where all this is leading?" Alex was giving her a chance to make a decision. Jessica understood that once she did there would be no turning back.

"I want you to be the first." She rested her face against his neck. "And I want you to be the last."

She had expected him to stiffen, to pull away and set her gently back in the water. Instead he tightened his hold on her. "I can't promise you that, Jessie. You can't go into this expecting a long-term love affair. I don't want a serious relationship. I've never had one, and I don't want one now. Not even with you."

"What do you want?"

"I want to make us both happy. I want to teach you about your body and watch your face when you find pleasure for the first time. I want to take you upstairs to that ridiculous bed and spend the rest of this evening making love to you."

"And later?"

"Later will take care of itself."

"How many women have you asked the same thing of?" Jessica tried to pull away, but Alex refused to let her.

"Not nearly as many as your imagination tells you I have. You're not one of a crowd, Jessie. There's never been anyone more special."

"And when I stop being special?"

"You'll always be special. When this relationship is over, I can promise I'll try very hard not to hurt you."

"And you're sure that this relationship will end, aren't you? You won't give it a chance for more."

"There's no chance," Alex said, his voice grave. "I don't want a wife, I don't want a family."

"So when you're through with me, you'll let me down easily." She pushed against his chest and this time he let her go. She stood in front of him. "You'll work hard to be sure I'm not too damaged. What part of yourself will you withhold so that I never know the real Alex Grainger?"

"You're still the same serious Jessica Cassidy." There was no humor in his words. She knew he wished she had changed that part of her, too. For Alex, the metamorphosis was incomplete.

"I'm afraid so. You can see, can't you, how impossible this is? I'm willing to take a chance on love and on my first lover, but not with the odds you've given me." Jessica turned and found the steps out of the tub. In a minute she had clasped her robe around her and tied the belt. "I'll be ready to go in a few minutes. The night's still young. I'm sure you can find someone else to share it with you."

Upstairs she took her clothes into the bathroom and

changed back into them. She pulled a brush through her wet hair and waited until her hands were no longer shaking before she went back down to join Alex. He had dressed, too, and silently he ushered her out of the house.

They were almost to the Bancrofts' before Alex spoke. "The day I saw you walking up the path of Ben and Lydia's house, I knew I was in trouble, Jessie. It had never occurred to me that I might want you. I never meant to take advantage of whatever youthful admiration you still had left for me, and I never meant to destroy the friendship of a lifetime."

"I know."

"But things are different than I thought they'd be. I do want you. More than I can say."

"Knowing that doesn't make me happy. I used to think it would." Jessica couldn't bear to look at him.

"I want you to think about what happened tonight. I'll stay away for a while and give you time to decide if you're sure you made the right choice."

"I don't need time to think, Alex. I don't see any one-night stands in my future. Not now. Not ever. Not even with you."

Alex pulled his car into the Bancrofts' driveway and stopped. "I never said anything about a one-night stand. I'm not putting a limit on our time together. I'm just telling you that it will end, and you should be prepared for that."

"Is this a standard contract you sign with all your lovers?"

His response was unexpected. His hand closed gently on the back of her neck and he pulled her to face him. "There's nothing standard about it." She shut her eyes as he bent to find her lips, brushing them sweetly in an old-fashioned kiss. "There's nothing standard about you."

When he released her, Jessica opened the car door. "Please don't come in." He nodded and she closed the door, standing to the side of the driveway as he backed out.

He had been gone for a long time before she turned and found her way through the trees to the house.

Chapter Seven

"The Kramers are begging me to persuade you to stay here and open a piano studio." Lydia dried and polished the stainless steel frying pan that Jessica had just washed. The pan gleamed from the effort.

"The Kramers. Are those the parents of Molly's friend, Patty?" Jessica unsuccessfully searched for more dishes to do.

"That's right. And you know they're not the first people who've asked what your plans are. If you announced that you were going to have a studio here, you'd have enough students to fill it before the words were out of your mouth. With us at the head of the list, naturally."

Jessica tried to smile at Lydia's enthusiasm. "There does seem to be a real need. I was even approached by a woman in town yesterday who'd heard I was a piano teacher. She said that she's been trying to find someone to teach her children for a year now."

Her words trailed off as she stared out the window at the bright morning sunlight, forgetting to drain the sink.

Staying in Lindleton and opening a studio weren't new ideas. She had come to love the little town, and she knew that she could be happy living there. The Bancrofts had become as close as family. Jessica knew that they'd be available to help her get started and to offer her friendship whenever she needed it. The town did have a real shortage of music teachers, and she would have no problem gathering students. Financially she was in the position of being able to move anywhere she wanted and buy a home of her own. There was only one problem: Alex Grainger.

Lydia put her arm around Jessica's waist and plunged her own hand into the soapy water to find the sink stopper. "I'm sure it's not an easy decision. But if you weren't happy here, you could move after you'd given it a fair chance."

"I don't know what to do," Jessica admitted. "I'm glad I've got some more time to think about it."

"You know you're welcome to stay here as long as you'd like. There's no hurry at all. We're glad to have you."

Jessica knew that Lydia meant her words, but she also knew that her own decision to leave or stay in Lindleton would be made by the end of the summer. She had to find out if she could live in the same town with Alex, breathe the same air, drink from the same water supply and know all the time that he was only a short distance away.

Lydia read her mind. "Alex is the problem, isn't he?"

Jessica felt that she could talk to Lydia about almost anything. The exception was men and Alex in particular. Jessica hadn't seen him since the abortive night in the hot tub two weeks before, but she knew that anything she could say to Lydia would only increase Lydia's unreasonable fears. She was saved from having to answer the question when Molly came into the kitchen.

"Dad says he can't find his blue tie with the little red and yellow stars on it. He wants you to come and help," Molly told her mother. "My advice is not to look very hard. It should stay lost."

"I already packed it," Lydia said. "I packed for both of us this morning before breakfast. I don't know how your father missed the suitcases sitting in the hallway."

"Go tell him," Jessica said with a pat on Lydia's shoulder and a friendly push. "I'll finish up in here."

"Do you know that this is the first time in years that Mom and Dad have gone away together?" Molly asked Jessica after her mother had left the room. "It's a miracle."

"Well, you're both old enough now for her to feel safe if she leaves for a little while."

"It's not that. It's you."

"I'm glad she trusts me to look out for things while she's gone." Jessica wiped the counter and then washed and dried her hands.

"Has she said anything about not letting me see Mike while she and Dad are away?"

"Not really."

"Don't ask! Please don't ask, Jessica."

Jessica groaned and threw the dish towel at Molly.

"You're going to turn my hair gray before they get back."

"They're only going to be gone for three days. Nothing can happen in three days," Molly pleaded.

Jessica remembered only too well what it was like to have parents who sheltered and overprotected their little girl. The boys hadn't exactly knocked down the Cassidys' door to get to Jessica, but when she had been asked out, her parents had investigated each young man so blatantly that Jessica had finally begun to turn down all invitations just to save herself the embarrassment. She had great affection and respect for Lydia. But in this one area, Jessica knew that Lydia had a blind spot that could eventually damage her daughter.

"I won't mention anything," Jessica promised reluctantly. "But if she tells me—on her own—that you're not to see Mike while she's gone, then I'll have to abide by her decision."

"Maybe you could sort of avoid her until she's all ready to go?"

Jessica shook her head at Molly, but her words were more positive. "I'll be in the music room if anyone needs me. I think I've got some very heavy practicing to do."

"Be sure to start with your D Major scale in triplets. Three octaves," Molly advised, tongue in cheek. Her eyes were alive with the happy possibility that she might soon be reunited, even temporarily, with Mike.

"It's going to take more than a D Major scale to make me feel like I'm doing the right thing." Jessica smiled to soften her words. She was uncertain about her decision, but Molly's eyes were too bright for Jessica to spoil her excitement.

The inevitable question came that night as Jessica and Molly prepared a simple supper of hamburgers and mashed potatoes. Lydia and Ben had been gone for hours.

"Jessica, Mike's invited me to a party tomorrow night. It's at a friend's summer cottage out in the country. Her parents are going to be there, and I have their number if you'd like to call and check it out." Molly whipped the potatoes with undisguised emotion. Jessica knew Molly was afraid she'd say no.

"What's your curfew?"

"Eleven-thirty. I think Mom is afraid if I stay out until midnight, I'll turn into a pumpkin."

"If it sounds all right after I call your friend's parents, then you can go. But you'll need to be home by eleven-thirty."

"That's not a problem. Mike's always been careful about getting me home on time."

Jessica wondered if there was more to the Molly-Mike saga than Molly had told her. She probed a little. "Did anything happen when you were dating Mike that would make your mother worry so much about him?"

Molly shook her head. Her usual pleasant face was compressed into a frown. "Nothing I can think of. Everything was going fine. Mom and Dad seemed to like him—there's no reason not to like Mike—but as soon as I started dating him steadily, Mom refused to let me go out with him anymore."

"How about your dad?"

"Dad told me not to push Mom. He said she'd

come around, and in the meantime it would be good for me to date other guys. But I don't want to date other guys. I just want to date Mike."

Jessica turned the hamburgers and sprinkled salt and pepper on them. "You are pretty young to be going steady."

"We're not that serious. I'm not thinking about getting married or even wearing his ring. I just like being with him, and right now no one else interests me." Molly put her hands on her hips and faced Jessica. "Now doesn't that sound pretty levelheaded to you?"

Jessica had to admit that it did. Everything about Molly was "levelheaded." She was intelligent, sensitive and more mature than any sixteen-year-old Jessica had ever met. At that moment, with her hands on her hips and her chin lifted defiantly, she resembled her mother so strongly that Jessica could almost imagine that she was looking at Lydia. And that was obviously the problem. Lydia looked at her daughter and saw herself at the same age. And whatever had happened to Lydia as a teenager still affected her.

"It makes sense to me," Jessica admitted. "Just don't put me in the middle of this, Molly. I'll let you go out with Mike while your parents are gone because I'm supposed to be using my own good judgment. But when they come back, please don't make a point of telling them that I let you go. It won't change your mother's mind and it might make her angry at us both."

"If she asks?"

"You'll have to tell the truth, of course."

As close as the members of the Bancroft family

were, both Clancy and Molly obviously enjoyed having their parents gone. It was a chance to break established routines and kick up their heels. Jessica was equally sure that Lydia and Ben were enjoying the same freedom.

After the dinner dishes were finished, Jessica piled the kids into her car and took them to Lindleton's one drive-in to see a double feature of space war movies. After several galaxies were destroyed and several more were saved, they found a hamburger stand that was still open and ordered giant milkshakes.

The next morning everyone, including Jessica, slept late. It was nearly lunchtime before they greeted the new day. The afternoon was spent just as lazily, and it was time for Molly to leave for her party before Jessica knew it.

"Eleven-thirty," she called to Molly and Mike as they walked hand in hand down the path to the driveway.

"No problem," Mike assured her. "We'll see you then."

Jessica watched them drive away with a trace of envy. She had kept herself busy during the past two weeks, making sure that she didn't have time to think about Alex. Now she was faced with a quiet evening she didn't want. What she wanted was to be going somewhere with the man she loved. Watching Molly walk away with her boyfriend increased Jessica's own loneliness.

"Clancy?" she called, when she was back inside. Perhaps Clancy would want to do something. If all else failed, Jessica knew she could suggest that they go to the Pizza Stop.

She found him upstairs throwing jeans into a backpack. "Mark invited me over to spend the night," he announced. "I can go, can't I?"

Scratch one boy companion. "I guess so. Just leave me the phone number."

"It's on the wall in the kitchen."

"Want me to drive you?" Jessica asked hopefully. At least it would give her something to do for a few minutes.

"He only lives three houses away."

"That's right." She cast about for something else. "Why don't I take you and Mark to the Pizza Stop for ice cream. Then I can drop you off at his house later."

"You need a boyfriend, Jessica." Clancy balled up the old Penn State sweatshirt that he always slept in and threw it in the backpack. "When you start asking two teenage boys to go out for ice cream, watch out."

Transparent, even to a fourteen-year-old. "You're right," she acknowledged. "Want to come, anyway?"

"Yeah. But it's a major sleepover at Mark's house, so there'll be about six other guys there. Can we all go?" He looked up and flashed Jessica a big grin.

"Not a chance."

"See you later, then." Clancy stopped at the door and winked. For a moment Jessica got a clear view of what the future Clancy Bancroft would look like. Watch out, Lindleton!

"Have a good time," she called to the sound of retreating footsteps.

Then she was alone.

The very worst thing about being lonely, she decided an hour after, was knowing that she didn't have to be. She could pick up the telephone, call Alex and instantly cure her loneliness. Cure was the wrong word, however, because it wouldn't be a cure, it would only be a temporary remission. Eventually she would be lonelier than ever.

Alex wanted her in his life, in his bed, but only on a temporary basis. He refused to consider the possibility of a relationship that was more involving. During the past two weeks she had experienced moments of doubt about her own need for something more satisfying than a short-term love affair. She had wondered if a lifetime of holding back emotionally was making her too careful, too puritanical.

In the end, however, she had known she was right. She was making no judgments about the way other people conducted their lives, but Jessica Cassidy had to do what was right for her. And giving herself to Alex, body, mind and spirit, with the sure knowledge that he was not giving the same, would be more pain than she could cope with. Being protected from life was wrong. Protecting yourself from heartbreak made good sense.

"Why did I fall in love with a man who doesn't understand the word?" she asked herself at eleven o'clock. She was curled up on the sofa watching a movie that insisted on making her cry. The worst thing was that she wasn't even sure the movie was supposed to be sad. She suspected that it wasn't. Still, she kept having to wipe her eyes.

She had fallen in love with Alex as a teenager. He had been everything she was not: carefree, happy, charming, lovable. She had talked herself out of her infatuation as she matured, but then she had succumbed to it again as soon as she was face-to-face with him. Why?

He was still carefree, happy, charming and lovable. So were plenty of other men who had wanted her. Why Alex Grainger? Because he was unattainable? She didn't think so. Because he was a symbol of her metamorphosis, the ultimate proof that she had become an attractive woman? No, that was too simple.

The truth was even simpler and harder to face. She was in love with Alex Grainger because he was Alex. And she wanted him for that reason. No other. Despite his faults, despite his philandering, despite his refusal to make a commitment.

By eleven-thirty, tears had given way to peace. The nagging doubt that she was doing the wrong thing had disappeared. Somewhere along the way Alex's attitude had to be challenged. Women were not toys to play with and abandon when he tired of them. If nothing else ever came out of their relationship, at least she could give Alex something to think about.

Jessica stood and went into the bathroom to wash her face. She combed her hair and decided that the damage to her eyes was minimal. Molly probably wouldn't notice she had been crying. Suspecting that the teenager would want to stay up and talk when she got home in a few minutes, Jessica went into the kitchen to pop corn.

The melted butter had congealed on the popcorn by eleven forty-five, and Jessica was beginning to worry. Molly had assured her that they wouldn't be late. Mike had assured her that they wouldn't be late. By five minutes to twelve, Jessica was in need of new assurances. She dialed the number of the girl whose party Molly and Mike were attending.

By the time she hung up the phone, Jessica was really worried. Molly and Mike had been at the party, but they had left quite a while before. Molly's friend couldn't understand why they weren't home yet.

Jessica was torn between going out to look for them, and staying by the telephone in case Molly called. By twelve-fifteen she was frantic.

"If this is what it's like to have kids," she fumed, "I think I'll just raise goldfish." She had begun pacing the floor by the telephone, stopping every few seconds to be sure that the sound of her footsteps wasn't masking the telephone's ring. "Where could they be?"

At twelve-thirty, Jessica gave up all semblance of good sense. Visions of Molly eloping ran through her head along with visions of Molly in trouble somewhere. Perhaps Mike wasn't the nice boy he seemed. Perhaps he had gotten angry with Molly and left her by the side of the road to walk home.

Waiting for the phone to ring seemed too torturous to bear, but Jessica knew that she would have little chance of finding Molly on the rural roads of the county. She had a vague idea where the party had been located, but no idea in the world of how to get there, much less how to retrace Molly's path. The only possibility of success would be to go with someone who knew his way around. Someone like Alex Grainger.

Without giving herself time to consider the problems that calling Alex could create, Jessica dialed his number. The phone seemed to ring forever before

Alex picked it up. Jessica wondered just what he had been doing. Sharing his hot tub with another woman? Sharing the massive bed with...

"Hello, Alex? It's Jessica."

"You pick interesting times to call, don't you?"

"Do I?" she snapped. Her concern for Molly sent her self-control flying out the window. "Is it an interesting time? It wouldn't be for most people, but then we never know about you, do we?"

There was a silence on the line. Jessica bit her bottom lip in frustration. Finally Alex answered. "Did you call to find out what I was doing? I was sleeping. Alone, I might add."

"I'm sorry," she apologized. This was no time to sound like a jealous shrew. "I didn't call to run a morals check. I called because I'm alone here. Ben and Lydia are out of town, Molly is an hour late coming from a date with Mike, and I'm worried sick. I need your help."

There was another long silence. Jessica bit her lip again.

The Alex who finally spoke was the one who behaved like a big brother. "Jessie, didn't I tell you not to get involved in the issue of Molly and Mike?"

"I don't want a lecture. I want your help."

Alex gave a tired sigh. "I'll be there in a few minutes." The line went dead.

Jessica ran upstairs to change out of her bathrobe and pajamas. By the time Alex arrived she was back downstairs dumping the popcorn in the kitchen wastebasket. She had already put coffee on to perk.

"Let's hear the whole story," Alex said in greeting. In spite of her fears about Molly, Jessica couldn't ignore the thrill that passed through her at seeing him again. He was dressed casually, as always, but his hair was still rumpled from sleep, and he was beginning to look as if he needed a shave. How could a man have eyes that green and clear even though he'd just gotten out of bed?

"I'm waiting." Alex poured himself a cup of coffee and sat on a kitchen stool.

Jessica explained the story without taking her eyes off him once. Alex in person was much harder to resist than the Alex she had lectured herself about all night. She wanted to run to him and put her arms around him for comfort. She wanted to bury her head in his shoulder and feel his whole body against hers.

"You blew it," he said when she had finished.

"Hindsight is wonderful."

"A little foresight would have been wonderful in this case. What did you expect to prove? That Molly and Mike could be trusted? Somewhere deep inside her, Lydia knows they can, Jessie. It doesn't help."

Jessica wanted him to understand. "You don't know what it's like having parents who wrap you in cotton gauze and keep you from making your own mistakes. I do, and I guess I let my own experience overshadow my good sense."

"Have you tried to call Mike's parents?"

Jessica nodded. "There was no answer."

"What do you want me to do?"

"I want to look for Molly, but I don't know where to go. Will you come with me?"

"Shouldn't someone be home to answer the phone if she calls?"

"I've got the Bancrofts' answering machine on

with instructions for Molly to leave a message. No one else would be calling this time of night.''

"Let's go, then.''

The northwestern Pennsylvania countryside was not welcoming in the darkness. The moon was only a faint crescent, and every shadow looked forbidding. Alex shook his head when Jessica told him where the party had been held. As they covered mile after mile, she could understand why. She had not realized that Molly and Mike would be so far away.

They followed the straightest route to the site of the party and then crisscrossed their path on less direct roads. An hour later they were back at the Bancrofts' house. There had been no sign of Molly or Mike.

"What if they eloped?'' Even saying the words out loud made Jessica want to cry.

"Let's not jump to conclusions.''

"It's hardly a jump, Alex. She's over two hours late.''

"But she's not so desperate to be with Mike that she'd want to marry him. She's still a kid.''

"When you were sixteen, did you feel like a kid? I didn't.''

"How did you feel?'' They had gone into the living room to wait and Alex pulled her down on the sofa beside him.

"I felt like a woman. A woman willing to do anything for the man she loved.''

"And who was the lucky man?''

"You.''

Alex tightened his arm around her, but he didn't say anything.

"Molly's so much more mature than I was, so much more sophisticated, but if she feels any of the same things I felt, well, who knows?"

"And what do you feel now?"

"I can't talk about that yet, Alex. Not with Molly missing."

"I've been giving you time."

"I know."

Alex stroked her hair and pulled her a little closer. "I'm not a patient man."

"I know that, too. You've never had to develop patience, have you?"

"Touché."

Jessica was achingly aware of Alex's body next to hers. Even with Molly on her mind, she couldn't ignore the sensations coursing through her bloodstream. Talking sense to herself couldn't begin to change what she felt for Alex. It could only change what she did about it.

Alex bent over and brushed his lips against hers, but before she could protest, he whispered, "You forgot to check for messages."

For a moment Jessica had been so lost in her feelings that she couldn't decipher Alex's sentence. Then she understood. She jumped up and ran to Ben's study to find the little red button on the message machine blinking merrily.

Alex stood in the doorway as she set the machine to play back. Molly's voice came over the speaker. "Jessica," she said slowly and distinctly, "I'm fine and I'm on my way home. Mike's car broke down and we had to walk a long way to get to a phone, but his uncle is coming to pick us up now. I should be home by two.''

"Thank God." Jessica turned off the machine and faced Alex. "She's all right."

"I thought she probably was, but I'm glad, too."

His words were interrupted by Molly's voice. "Jessica?" The front door slammed. Alex and Jessica went to the front hall to find her.

"I'm so sorry," Molly apologized before either of them could say a word. Jessica was delighted to see that Molly looked no worse for wear. An older man was standing at her side.

"I'm Mitchell Dempsey, Mike's uncle," he said, introducing himself. Alex and Jessica murmured their names and shook his hand. "The kids ended up at a farmhouse way out in God's country. I had a heck of a time finding them. I dropped Mike off at my house on the way in. They're both fine. Just exhausted."

"I am tired," Molly agreed. "We walked for miles and miles."

"They took the scenic route home," Mitchell explained. "When they broke down, they were right in the middle of a long stretch of Amish farmhouses. Since they knew that the Amish don't use modern equipment, when they saw their buggies outside they figured that there wouldn't be any phones. They just kept walking until they found a place where they could call."

"Run on up to bed," Jessica told Molly. "You can tell me the whole story tomorrow."

With a grateful smile, Molly went upstairs.

"Thank you so much, Mr. Dempsey," Jessica said.

"No problem. Mike stays with me a lot when his

folks are away on business. It's the first time he's ever given me cause to worry. I'm just glad they're both okay." With a smile and a "Good night," he was gone.

"Well, Jessie?" Alex said when they were alone again. "What now?"

"A big thank-you and a good night's sleep," she said.

"Not so fast."

Jessica couldn't pretend she didn't understand his words. "This is no time to talk. It's past 2:00 A.M."

"I'll pour you another cup of coffee, but you and I are going to settle this tonight."

She let him lead her back into the living room, and she sat quietly while he went into the kitchen. She had been putting off this scene, not because she had any doubts about her answer, but because it was so final. Now she wished she could put it off even longer.

"Here you go." Alex came back into the room and handed her a cup, which she set on the end table. He sat beside her. "I'm waiting," he said as she folded her hands in her lap and tried to decide how much to tell him.

"This isn't easy," she began.

"It doesn't have to be hard. Just tell me you've thought about us, and you've decided to..." Alex stopped as if his next words were awkward to say, even for him.

"Decided to have an affair? Decided to take a temporary lover?" Jessica put her head on the back of the sofa and closed her eyes. "I haven't decided any of those things, Alex. I'm not in the market for a fling, not even with you.''

''What does that mean? Not even with me?''

She was surprised by the warmth of his tone. This was Alex at his best. Patient, concerned, caring. It made what she had to say that much harder. She opened her eyes; it was not fair for either of them to hold back. At the very least they owed each other their real feelings.

''Not even with you,'' she repeated. ''I've been in love with you forever. Sure, I thought I'd grown out of it, that it was just a teenage crush, but then I discovered that the adult Jessica loves the adult Alex. I can't have an affair with you. If it hurts me to have you ask, what will it do to me when you leave?''

A shadow of pain crossed his face and Jessica reached up to smooth it away. ''I'm not angry at you,'' she said softly. ''But it seems to me that you should have learned by now what kind of women can handle your rules and what kind can't.''

''Believe me, this has been against my better judgment.'' Alex caught her hand and brought it to his mouth to kiss each fingertip. Then he held it to his cheek again. ''Who would have thought that little Jessica Cassidy could turn me inside out?''

Jessica understood that he was trying to lighten the tension, but she refused to let him. ''Turning you inside out is a good start. But can't you see that I need more? You need more?''

''I certainly need more.'' Alex pulled her arms around his neck and held her close. Jessica could feel her tears building at the sudden intimacy. ''I need all of you. Jessie, don't cut yourself off from me.''

"I won't let you use me and then discard me like a slightly soiled teddy bear." She put her hands against his chest and pushed to free herself.

"You've blown everything out of proportion." He let her go but his voice showed his irritation. "I'm tired of you making me sound like a selfish playboy. I wanted to give you good times. God knows, you need them badly after everything you've been through. Where's your sense of proportion?"

Jessica stared at him. She couldn't even make herself move away. "Good times? Until you stop being a good time man, Alex, you aren't even going to develop a sense of proportion."

His green eyes were clouded with anger. Jessica realized that it was the first time she had ever seen him so upset. Somehow it didn't frighten her. She only wanted to continue, to be finished with all that was between them so that they could both move ahead with their lives.

She took a deep breath. "No one's ever told you no, have they, Alex? Not in your entire life. Not your mother, not your father. No one. Well, let me be the first. I don't want your good times unless I can have all your times."

"I've told you that's impossible."

"Then get out of my life, Alex Grainger." Her own words had given her the strength to move completely away from him. Jessica stood and walked to the front door, flinging it open for his exit. "Take that small empty part of you that you allow a woman to fill, and find someone else to fill it for you."

Alex passed through the doorway in silence, but he turned on the front porch and faced her. "I misjudged you badly, Jessie. I thought you were grown up enough to handle this.''

"You did misjudge me. I'm much *too* grown up to handle it.''

He turned and without another word he disappeared through the trees. Jessica watched him go, only allowing herself the release of tears when the sound of the Porsche's engine had faded into the stillness of the night.

Chapter Eight

Jessica could feel the piano keys vibrate at the force of her touch. If she had ever doubted her ability to put all her strength into her fingertips, she no longer did. In the week since she had last seen Alex, she had played her entire repertoire with a passion that rivaled any concert artist's. This morning, after another sleepless night, she felt especially emotional.

"That was lovely. And very sad."

Jessica turned to find Lydia in the doorway of the music room. "Was I disturbing you?" Jessica asked. She had an unwelcome vision of waking up the entire household.

"Not at all. It's a wonderful way to wake up, although I'd like it better if I didn't think you were upset about something."

Jessica smiled ruefully. "My mother always said that she could tell what was going on inside me just by the pieces I chose to practice."

"Your mother must have been a sensitive woman."

"Well, I was pretty obvious. If I was angry I'd play the first movement of Beethoven's *Pathétique* Sonata over and over and over."

"And if you were happy?"

"Chopin waltzes, especially the one everybody calls the *Minute* Waltz. I'd play it as fast as I could until my fingers got all tangled on the keys and I had to stop."

"I haven't heard any waltzes."

"Someday I'll play them for you." Jessica stood, hoping that the conversation would end without Lydia asking her what was troubling her. She was still too raw to talk about Alex.

Instead, Lydia surprised her. "Jessica, I know that you let Molly date Mike while we were gone. If that's bothering you, please don't worry. I'm not upset about it."

"I'm glad. I realize I shouldn't have gone against your wishes."

"You were put in the middle, and you did what you thought was best. The middle is never an easy place to be." The smile that accompanied Lydia's words was reassuring.

"Molly wanted to go so badly, and she seems so responsible," Jessica explained. "Mike is such a nice boy." She wanted Lydia to understand. Maybe another perspective would help her realize that she was being too strict.

"Come help me get breakfast together and I'll tell you a story," Lydia said.

Jessica followed her into the kitchen and got bowls

and plates out of the cabinet to set the table. Lydia was quiet for a few moments, and then she began.

"Believe it or not, I was sixteen once. I wasn't as mature as Molly, but I was very much like her in other ways. I was romantic, innocent, trusting, just like Molly is. There was a boy in my classes who began to pay me a lot of attention. I was what you might call a late bloomer, and I didn't have a lot of boyfriends. When this boy began to act like he cared for me, I fell madly in love."

Jessica didn't want to break the flow of Lydia's words. She just nodded in response.

"My parents were so glad to see me dating that it never occurred to them that I might get in over my head. I began to go steady, and they never thought to stop me. I was very foolish. And later—" she paused as if to decide how to phrase the rest "—when I was seventeen, I paid a heavy price for my foolishness. The boy wasn't interested in me anymore after he took what he wanted, and I was left alone to pick up the pieces of my life."

Jessica waited until she was certain Lydia was finished. "And you're afraid Molly will get hurt, just like you did."

"That's right."

"It must be very difficult to watch your children make mistakes."

"It's the hardest thing in the world."

Jessica thought about her own experience waiting for Molly to return from her date. "I think I probably understand that a little better now, but I also understand something else." She turned to face Lydia. "Molly's not like you were at sixteen, and she's not like I was. She's intelligent and practical, and she has something that neither you nor I had at that age: confidence. Now you've got to have confidence in her." Jessica turned away, afraid to see the expression on Lydia's face. She had just given the older woman every reason to be angry at her.

"I know." Lydia's voice was gentle. She came up behind Jessica and put her hand on her shoulder. "Ben's been telling me the same thing for months. I realize now that you're both right. That's one reason I went away for a few days; I needed to think. But I told Molly last night that she can see Mike when she wants to, just as long as she follows the rules."

"She will." Jessica turned and tried to give Lydia a big smile. It felt strange; she hadn't smiled in days. "Thanks for understanding my interference."

"And now I'm going to interfere."

Jessica stiffened. She wasn't ready to talk about her feelings. Not even to this more understanding Lydia.

"You've been very unhappy, and I don't think it was just the situation with Molly, was it?"

Jessica shook her head.

Lydia tackled the problem head on. "Is Alex giving you trouble, Jessica?"

Jessica was tired. She had slept little in the past week. Her emotions were a tangled skein inside her, and her self-control was sitting on empty. The concern in the older woman's eyes was her undoing.

"You're not *my* mother, Lydia," she said, trying to keep her voice from breaking. "You can't fix what's wrong with me like you did with Molly. Please don't try." Before Lydia could respond, Jessica turned and fled the kitchen.

Later in her room, Jessica counted all the ways that she had failed since coming to Lindleton. Number one: she had allowed herself to fall back in love with Alex Grainger. Number two: she had allowed herself to get involved in a mother-daughter conflict that was none of her business. Number three: she had just permanently alienated Lydia, one of the best friends she'd ever had.

Hadn't she come to Lindleton to take a rest from emotional upheaval? Hadn't she come to spend a quiet summer thinking about her life and making plans for her future? If she had any sense she'd get up, pack and leave for Pittsburgh.

But then there was the one way she hadn't failed. She had taught two talented piano students to enjoy making music. She could not abandon Clancy and Molly. Children, even teenage children, believed that the world revolved around them. If she left precipitately, Clancy and Molly would blame her departure on themselves.

Still torn between running away and staying in Lindleton, Jessica was only sure of one thing. No matter what she decided, she knew that she owed Lydia an apology. Jessica found her in the kitchen, eating cereal by herself.

"May I say I'm sorry?" Jessica asked from the doorway. "I'm not used to sharing my feelings with anyone. I don't know how to do it very well."

Lydia looked up and Jessica saw that she had been crying. Jessica wanted to cry, too.

"I shouldn't have pushed you." Lydia tried to smile.

Jessica crossed the room and knelt beside Lydia to

hug her. "It was my fault, really. I've always kept my problems to myself, and I'm not used to talking about what's bothering me. Please forgive me for snapping at you like that."

"Of course I forgive you." Lydia put her own arms around Jessica.

"When it doesn't hurt so much, I'll tell you what's been bothering me," Jessica promised.

"You just tell me what you want, when you want to." Lydia straightened and put her hand under Jessica's chin to tilt her face to hers. "I know I can't replace your mother," Lydia said softly, "but if you ever need a good friend, I'm here."

Two weeks later Jessica twisted her hair into a knot high on her head and secured it with hairpins. She stood back from the mirror to view the entire effect. "What do you think?" she asked Molly.

"I think I'm going to let my hair grow so I can do the same thing." Molly came to the mirror and stood beside Jessica, squinting as she did so. "Look, our faces are the same shape. My hair would look good that way, too."

Jessica examined the younger girl's face in the mirror. "You're right." She squinted, too. "I never realized it, but you and I look a little bit alike."

Molly continued to compare them. "Same shape face, same color eyes, same funny eyebrows." She shook her head. "Different chins, though."

"Twins we're not," Jessica agreed. "But your hair would look good like this." She pulled the short strands back from Molly's face.

"I'll let it grow," Molly said decisively. "But today I'm going to have to settle for what I have."

"Are you girls ready?" Ben Bancroft's voice drifted up the stairwell.

"We're coming!" Molly yelled. She turned to Jessica. "I'm glad you decided to come to the picnic."

Every year for the past four decades, the first weekend in August had been the date of the annual Lindleton General picnic. This year the Bancrofts had invited Jessica to the festivities, and she had reluctantly agreed to go. It had been two weeks since she had seen Alex, and she was not sure that she was ready to face him yet. As if Ben understood her hesitancy, he mentioned casually that Alex probably wouldn't be able to attend since he was on call that weekend. Now, standing in front of the mirror and viewing the effect of a new apricot-colored sundress she had bought for the occasion, Jessica wished perversely that Alex was going to be there, after all. Let him see what he was missing.

The park where the hospital held the picnic included acres of woods with several large clearings and one regulation-size baseball diamond. A softball game was in progress when Ben Bancroft pulled the family station wagon into the parking lot and began to unload picnic baskets and folding chairs. In between their picnic table and the car, Jessica discovered that Alex was playing first base.

"What are you mumbling about?" Molly asked as she passed Jessica, whose pace had slowed to snail speed.

"My father always said to be careful about what you wish for. It might come true."

Molly cocked her head and frowned. "What's that supposed to mean?"

"It means that people aren't the best judges of what's good for them."

"I know that," Molly said with teenage disgust. "What's it got to do with you?"

But Jessica was staring at Alex, who had just turned to stare at her, and she didn't even hear Molly's question. Molly shook her head and walked away.

Jessica watched Alex find a substitute for first baseman. She waited quietly as he came to join her. Without a word he took her hand and led her to a small grove of trees where they could have some privacy.

"I was hoping you'd be here," he said, after she dropped his hand to lean against a tall sycamore.

"God help me, I was hoping you'd be here, too."

He lifted his hand again and brushed her cheek with his fingertips. Jessica closed her eyes. The reaction of her body was completely out of proportion to the gentle stroking.

"Jessie," Alex asked softly. "What are we going to do?"

"I thought I knew what I was going to do," she answered. "I guess I was fooling myself."

"Have you changed your mind, then?"

"No." She opened her eyes and found his. "Can't we give each other time?"

Alex looked doubtful. "Are you asking me to be a friend? To hold your hand when I want to hold your body next to mine?"

"I'm asking you to give us both time. If you feel anything for me other than desire…"

"You know I do!"

"Then, please, let's not ruin our friendship with demands neither of us can meet."

"You're fooling yourself." Alex's voice was a warm caress. "We'll spend time together, but it won't be enough for either of us. One or both of us will lose control and we'll be right back where we started. Only it will hurt worse."

"I'll take that chance." Jessica covered the slight distance between them and put her hands on his shoulders. "Will you?"

"You're bound and determined to teach me self-restraint, aren't you?"

"I've never thought that was my purpose in life."

"And what is your purpose?" Alex put his hands on her waist and drew her closer.

"I guess that's for both of us to decide." She lifted herself on her toes and found his lips with hers.

"Nice going, Jessica!" Clancy yelled behind her.

Jessica turned in Alex's arms and shot Clancy a smile. "Go away, kid. You bother me!"

"Didn't I tell you that you needed a boyfriend!" He grinned at them both and sauntered away.

"Sounds like Clancy's on my side," Alex said.

"Every man in the world thinks that a man is the solution to every woman's problems."

"Men are so wise."

Jessica pulled away and offered him her hand. She smiled but her heart wasn't in it. Nothing had been gained. Unfortunately Alex was correct. She was postponing the inevitable by dragging out the finale of their relationship. And yet, she couldn't seem to convince herself that goodbye was the only thing left for either of them to say. "I want to believe in miracles," she murmured.

"Jessie?"

She sighed. "I was just thinking out loud."

His hand around hers was warm and strong. "Let's give each other this day," he said softly. "With no strings attached."

The Bancrofts welcomed Alex into their midst as if he were a member of the family. He brought his own fast-food lunch to their table, but Lydia made him put it away, insisting that she had packed more than enough for all of them. They ate fried chicken and potato salad and, in that one sitting, demolished a devil's food cake that Clancy had baked. Afterward the adults sipped wine coolers and gossiped while Molly and Clancy went to find their friends.

Jessica was acutely aware of the effect that sitting next to Alex had on her nervous system. Was it possible, or was she imagining that he had grown even more attractive in the past weeks? His tan was darker, and she wondered what activities he had been pursuing in the sunshine. By contrast, his hair seemed more blond than brown, and his green eyes were more dominant. He seemed to be filled with restless energy, and though he had always been a person who liked touching others, now he seemed to crave the feel of her skin almost constantly.

She knew where it was all leading. Perhaps he had said that there were no strings attached to this day, but neither of them was going to be able to be "just friends" again. Every time he unconsciously stroked her arm or rubbed her bare back, he was making demands on her. Every time she felt her body respond, she knew that his demands would be harder to refuse than before.

"Let's go watch the tug-of-war," Lydia suggested, standing and motioning to Ben.

"Are you coming?" Ben asked Jessica and Alex.

Jessica thought it would be a good idea to stay busy. She stood and helped pull Alex to his feet. Alex's beeper sounded, as if it had been waiting for the activity to set it off.

Alex groaned and Ben laughed. "Better you than me," he commiserated. "There's a pay phone at the park entrance."

"I'll be back," Alex promised Jessica.

She watched him jog down the road before she caught up with Lydia and Ben.

"That's too bad," Lydia said. "Alex rarely has a moment to himself. Even Ben isn't as busy as Alex is."

"Why is that?" Jessica was genuinely curious. Alex had an associate. Ben was in his practice alone. And Ben was the only obstetrician in town.

"Because he's too dedicated," Ben answered decisively. "I've told him that to his face, so I'm not talking out of turn. Alex is absolutely zealous when it comes to the practice of medicine. He makes no compromises, accepts no limitations. He's made medicine his whole life."

"My good time man," Jessica said softly.

"On the surface he may seem carefree, but underneath is an almost obsessive need to be the best in his field." Ben laid his arm on Jessica's shoulders as if to comfort her. "I wonder sometimes if there's room for anything else in his life."

"So do I."

Alex returned only to leave twice more in the space of two hours. He grew more serious as the afternoon progressed, drawing Ben aside for a conference at one point. Although he still seemed to need Jessica by his side, he had become more distant until, when the beeper went off for the fourth time, she was almost glad to see him heading for the telephone.

When he returned there was no trace of the smiling Alex she knew and loved. "I have to go," he told her. "I've got a patient I have to see."

Jessica was disappointed, but she knew that she had lost his attention, anyway. Something else had taken priority. "I understand," she said.

"Will you come with me?"

The question was a surprise. She nodded, happy that even though he was preoccupied he wanted her company.

They were speeding down the road in his Porsche before he explained where they were going.

"Do you remember our dinner at the Ale 'n' Cow?"

Jessica nodded.

"Do you remember our discussion about fathers not being allowed in the delivery room at Lindleton General, and how Ben and I disagreed with the hospital's policy?"

She nodded again.

"Well, I've got a patient, a young woman just out of her teens who's been coming to me for prenatal care, who also disagrees with the policy. Janna decided that if her husband, Ken, wasn't allowed to be there, they'd have the baby at home. She went into labor early this morning, but they didn't call me until this afternoon."

"Surely they don't expect you to deliver the baby in their bedroom. Couldn't you be sued if there was a problem?" Jessica began to gnaw at her bottom lip.

"I could. Any number of things could happen to me. I explained all of that to them when they decided not to come in to the hospital. I really thought they understood and that they'd drive to one of the bigger cities to have the baby."

"And they didn't."

"Unfortunately they didn't. They're very much back-to-the-land kind of people. They have a little farm where they raise goats and chickens and vegetables. Some of their ideas are sound, and this one might not have been too bad except that at Janna's last appointment I discovered that the baby was breech."

"Didn't you tell her?"

"Of course. But they bought a book about delivering babies and they read that most babies turn in the last days before the onset of labor. According to Ken, there are all sorts of home remedies to avoid breech delivery." Alex slapped his hand on the steering wheel in a sudden burst of anger. "Those two fools are out at their place right now, refusing to come into town and have the baby at the hospital."

"And you're going there to deliver it?" Jessica was aghast.

"I'm going there to drag them both into town. By now, Janna will probably have to have a caesarean, and that's something I don't do. As soon as I can convince them to go to the hospital, I'll have Ben meet us there. I've already filled him in.''

Alex sped over the county's paved and unpaved roads until they came to a turnoff that thwarted even the Porsche. They crept along, slowing even more for bumps and ruts.

''There's the house,'' Alex said, nodding to a weathered brown frame shack sitting at the end of the drive.

''How did you find it?''

''I've been here for dinner. Janna makes the best vegetarian lasagna in the world.''

Jessica processed the new piece of information. ''Do they pay their bills with eggs and bushels of corn?''

''And vegetarian lasagna.'' Alex threw his door open and covered the distance to the house in a sprint. Jessica followed close behind.

''How's she doing?'' Alex asked a young man who had come out on the porch to greet them.

The young man shrugged, but the lines of concern etched on his face belied the casual response. ''It's not as easy as the book made it sound,'' he admitted in a low tone.

Alex pushed past him and went into the house. Jessica stayed on the porch. She introduced herself to Ken and then both of them waited quietly for sounds from the house. There was a muffled scream, and then, nothing.

''I've been trying to get her to go to the hospital since lunchtime,'' Ken said, staring straight ahead. ''She just kept refusing, said it was natural to have a hard time with the first baby.''

Jessica found it difficult to offer comfort. Although Ken and Janna had acted from their idealism, they had endangered their baby's life. She did the best she could. "Calling Dr. Grainger was a good idea."

"Janna's going to be angry. She doesn't know I called."

"Perhaps it's time to begin thinking about what's best and not about what Janna wants," Jessica said. "It's your baby, too."

Alex slammed the door behind them, and both Ken and Jessica jumped.

"She's not in good shape," Alex said bluntly. "It's been a fast labor, she's almost completely dilated but the baby's still turned and there's no way I can deliver it safely here. I've called an ambulance, but Janna's refusing to go. Go in there and tell her she's going, anyway."

"I don't know," Ken said.

"You'd better know!" Alex grabbed Ken by the arms and turned him around. "You want the whole truth, Ken? I don't know if we're going to be able to save the baby as it is. Do you want to lose them both?"

Ken's face drained of all color. "No!"

"Then, damn it, act like a father and a husband instead of a child!" Alex went back inside and Ken followed. Jessica could hear the murmur of voices, and finally after what seemed an eternity, she heard the siren of an ambulance.

The young woman who was carried past her on a stretcher was too pale to be alive, although her eyes were open and her head turned side to side in pain. Jessica ached to comfort her, but she stayed back until the ambulance roared away with Alex, Janna and Ken riding in the back. Alex had given Jessica the keys to his Porsche with instructions to drive it to his house. There hadn't even been time for a goodbye.

With great care she steered the powerful sports car back along the potholed drive and then over the country roads until she reached Alex's house. Once there, she tried the garage door, found it unlocked and parked the car. She experimented with the rest of the keys on Alex's key chain until she found the one that led inside. Settling herself on a big sofa near the infamous hot tub, she waited for Alex.

The house was silent, no clocks ticked, no pets rustled through the rooms. She was struck with how secluded it was, and she wondered if Alex ever felt lonely. She wondered if he was home alone often enough to care.

The unearthly quiet began to lull her senses. Jessica shut her eyes and snuggled into the soft cushions. She fell asleep thinking of Alex's arms around her. She awoke to the real thing.

"Jessie."

She turned and reached for Alex to pull him closer. It seemed perfectly natural to be lying against him with her head in the crook of his shoulder. "I fell asleep."

"I know."

Jessica was puzzled by the tone of his voice. He sounded different. "When did you get back?"

"Just a few minutes ago."

She was still disoriented, but she was slowly remembering why she was there. "The baby," she asked softly. "Did the baby come?"

She felt him nod.

Now she was fully awake and icy fingers of fear tugged at her. "Is the baby all right?"

Alex pulled her closer. "No," he said, his voice breaking.

"Oh, no!" She was so wrapped in her own grief that for a moment she failed to perceive his. Then she realized that Alex was crying. "I'm so sorry," she whispered, trying to soothe him. "I'm so sorry."

She could feel his rigid body shake with the sobs he gave way to and the sobs he still repressed. She held him, rubbing his back and murmuring words of sympathy until finally he was quiet. "Do you want to talk about it?" she asked.

He was silent for a long time, but she could feel his body begin to relax against hers. Finally, with one hand he pulled the pins from her hair and spread the auburn wealth of it over both of them like a cloak. "Ben thinks the baby died early in labor. Long before they even called me. I knew we'd lost him as soon as I examined Janna."

Jessica was relieved that Alex couldn't blame himself, but his next words quelled her relief.

"It was my fault."

"How can you say that?" she asked.

"I should have demanded that Janna go into the hospital. I should have threatened her, browbeat her, begged her. I should have gotten her in somehow."

"She's an adult and so is Ken. You can't force adults to do anything, Alex. Surely you know that's true."

"All I know is that I lost a beautiful little boy today."

"Is Janna all right?" She was desperate to make him aware of the good he had done.

"She's distraught, but physically she's going to be fine."

"If you hadn't gone out there today and insisted she go to the hospital, she might have died, too. Ken was too confused to make the decision himself. No other doctor I know would have cared that much." Jessica moved against the back of the sofa so that she could see Alex's face. Her fingers traced the path of his tears. "You did all you could. All anyone could."

"And I failed."

"You're wrong." Jessica watched him try to accept what she was saying. At that moment, she loved him more than she had known she could love anyone. This was Alex, her good time man. This was the man who wanted no ties and nothing but the physical delights of a relationship. And yet, he had come to her when he needed comfort. He had come to her to share his sorrows.

As if he, too, was aware of the importance of the moment, he stroked her hair and tried to smile. "What would I have done if you weren't here?"

She wanted to tell him that she'd always be there if he wanted her. Instead she tried to smile back. "I'm very glad I was."

"So am I, Jessie." He kissed her and she could taste the salt of his tears. "So am I."

Chapter Nine

Jessica spread a quilt on the grassy expanse behind the Bancrofts' house and lay down on her stomach, propping her chin on folded hands. The sun was high in the sky, and even though the day was overcast, she could feel a pleasant heat on her bare legs and arms. The book she had brought to read lay untouched by her side and the radio she had brought to listen to was silent.

The eighteenth of August was always a time of contemplation for Jessica. It was a time to sum up the year, to meditate on her successes and her failures. It was her birthday.

The Cassidys had viewed birthdays as important rites of passage. Birthdays were formal times usually celebrated by a trip to a good restaurant for loving lectures on how Jessica could do better the next year. She rarely had a party, but there was always a special present and the rare privilege of having a friend over to spend the night.

The habit of self-examination was a hard one for Jessica to break. The past year had been the most difficult of her life, but now she did not dwell on her parents' deaths. She had said her goodbyes to them and moved ahead. Instead she found herself concentrating on her future. In two weeks, Clancy and Molly would begin school, and there would be no more time for intensive music study. It was time for Jessica to move ahead again.

She was no closer to making a decision about what to do than she had been weeks before. Her relationship with Alex was no closer to being resolved; in fact, she hadn't seen or heard from him in the past week.

She thought of the last time she had seen him. They had gone together to the funeral for Janna and Ken's baby. Alex had held her hand tightly as the old country preacher droned on about angels and cherubs and playgrounds in heaven. They had offered words of condolence and driven home in a silence that neither of them wanted to break. Alex had kissed her at the front door, and the kiss had gone on and on until Jessica had felt her own tears slip down her cheeks.

She had hoped that sharing their sorrow would bring them closer, but as if he was afraid he was being trapped by the emotional link between them, Alex had stayed away. Ben reported that Alex seemed to be working harder than ever, as if the death of the baby was driving him to be even more dedicated. And it was only from Ben that she learned that the board of Lindleton General, influenced by the tragedy, had finally decided to change its policy of not allowing fathers to witness their babys' births.

Although Alex knew that Jessica would be leaving Lindleton soon, there had been no indication from him that he wanted her to stay. If she remained in town, bought a house and opened a piano studio, it would be with no hope that Alex wanted a permanent relationship. Under the circumstances, it made sense for her to go back to Pittsburgh, sell her parents' house and buy something smaller and more suitable for a single woman. She could find music students in the city, and the opportunities for a social life would be greater.

"I know a secret!"

Lost in thought, Jessica hadn't heard Molly come up behind her. Now she turned and smiled at the teenager, patting the place beside her on the quilt. "Come join me."

"You looked so serious I almost hated to interrupt."

"I was just deciding what to do with my life."

"That's easy. Stay here."

"What's your secret?"

Molly made a face at Jessica's slick change of subject. "If I tell you, it won't be a secret."

"Tell me and then we'll keep it a secret from someone else."

"I don't think so." Molly couldn't resist adding, "But you'll like this secret."

"If I keep probing I'll have it out of you in the space of another heartbeat."

"Not a chance!" Molly rolled over on her side and watched Jessica. "Why don't you stay in Lindleton, Jessica? I don't want you to go away. I love you."

Jessica was consistently amazed at how free the

Bancroft family felt to express affection. She had always known that her own parents loved her, but she could count on the fingers of one hand the number of times they had told her so. "I love you, too, Molly. You're like the sister I always wanted and never had. Even if I leave, I promise I'll stay in touch. And you can come down to Pittsburgh and visit me."

Molly was pouting. "That won't be the same thing at all."

"Please don't think this has anything to do with you. Lindleton just may not be the best place for me to settle."

"It's Alex's fault. I'm going to punch him in the nose at dinner." Molly clapped her hand over her mouth. "Whoops!"

"What else are you trying not to tell me?"

"I'm leaving before I say another word." Molly stood. "Don't try to pump me for information," she said, dramatically rolling her eyes. "You know too much already!"

Just why would Alex be coming to dinner? Jessica lay on her back with her arm over her eyes to block the sun. She wondered fleetingly if somehow the Bancrofts had discovered that today was her birthday. It might be possible that Alex remembered the date, but it was extremely unlikely. He had never celebrated it with her, although she remembered that on her fifteenth birthday he had been present at the country club when a big cake with a sparkler on it had been brought to her parents' table. Alex's presence in the room had been the most exciting thing about the day.

No, Alex wouldn't remember the date. But his mother might have remembered and written him, though that, too, was unlikely. He must be coming for another reason. Whatever it was, she would find out soon enough.

Jessica was trying to decide what to wear for dinner when Lydia came to stand in the open doorway. "Jessica?"

"Hi. Where have you been all day?"

"Doing errands," Lydia said, with a disgusted expression. "And do you know what? I didn't get finished. I still forgot to pick up Ben's suit from the cleaner, and he has to have it tomorrow. Would it be too much of an imposition to ask you to run into town and get it for me?"

"No problem at all. Maybe Molly would like to go, too."

"I don't think so," Lydia said vaguely. "She said something about having other plans."

Jessica wondered if Lydia knew that Alex had mysteriously been invited to dinner, but she refrained from mentioning it. "I'll be ready to leave in a few minutes."

Jessica changed into a lilac cotton sweater and skirt and brushed her hair before going to find Lydia. Lydia looked even more harried than before. "Jessica, I promised Ben I'd make his favorite artichoke dip to go with dinner tonight, and I'm completely out of canned artichokes. Will you stop by the grocery store on the way back?"

"Certainly." Jessica waited while Lydia made a quick list that contained more than artichokes. "Anything else?"

"Well, Clancy did ask me to drive by the movie

theater and find out what's going to be playing tomorrow, but you don't have to go out of your way.''

"I don't mind.''

"You're such a sweetheart.'' Lydia gave her an affectionate hug. "We'll see you later.''

In Lindleton, Jessica was amazed at how much traffic a little town could produce. Since it was Friday afternoon, everyone seemed to be going somewhere for the weekend. There were cars backed up at every stoplight, and even the sidewalks were crowded with shoppers. At the dry cleaner's a long line stretched out the door; at the grocery store every checkout had at least four customers. And, as if the town had conspired to make her trip as difficult as possible, the street in front of the movie theater was being repaired. Jessica had to park her car several blocks away and hike the distance to read the billboard in front of it.

"All that for *Terrible Tales of Terror*,'' she muttered as she crossed the street to get back in her car. "If Clancy sees that he won't sleep for a week.''

Alex's Porsche was comfortably settled in the Bancrofts' driveway when Jessica pulled in. She parked to the side and then gathered Ben's suit and the bag of groceries. No matter what his reason was for being there, Jessica was thrilled to know that she would be with Alex on her birthday. Even if she was the only one who knew how special the day was.

The front door was locked, an unusual occurrence, and Jessica rang the doorbell. When no one answered she hung Ben's suit on the light fixture beside the door and dug for her key. Inside, the house appeared to be deserted. "Anybody home?'' she called. Shrugging her shoulders she retrieved the suit and stepped inside. She was on her way to the kitchen to find Lydia when she heard a giggle from behind the closed dining room door.

"Molly?"

There was no answer. Suspicious and curious at the same time, Jessica pushed the door open.

"Surprise!"

"Surprise!"

The dining room, usually reserved for formal occasions, had been transformed into a wonderland of bright balloons and crepe paper streamers. Signs proclaiming Happy Birthday, Jessica were plastered on every wall, and the table was set with the Bancrofts' finest china and silver. Alex and the entire Bancroft family were wearing silly party hats, and at Jessica's arrival they began to sing. "Happy Birthday to you, Happy Birthday to you…"

Jessica was stunned, and she stood, rooted to the spot, while the off-key serenade continued. When they had finished she was bombarded with hugs and good wishes and drawn into the room.

"How did you know?" she asked, choking on the tears building inside her.

"I remembered," Alex said. He leaned over to kiss her cheek. "Happy Birthday, Jessie."

"But you couldn't have remembered!"

Alex gestured around the room. "Proof."

"We fixed all your favorite foods," Molly said, her eyes sparkling. "And we're going to play all your favorite music during dinner, and we're going to have your favorite cake."

"Yeah, and afterward you get to open your presents," Clancy broke in. "The rest is nothing."

"Thank you all, " Jessica said, trying hard not to cry. There was so much good feeling in the room. She had never felt so surrounded by warmth and love. Against her will she compared it to her quiet birthday celebrations as a child. This was the party she had always dreamed about.

"Here's your hat," Molly said, pushing the shiny silver cone on Jessica's head and snapping a piece of elastic under her chin. "And here's your place." Jessica was escorted to the head of the table, where Ben usually sat.

"Are you sure?" she asked Ben.

"Family tradition," he assured her. "You're being treated to a real Bancroft celebration. We consider you part of the clan."

"I can't think of anything nicer," she said sincerely.

The dinner progressed just as Molly had promised. It seemed that everyone had been watching her for weeks, trying to figure out what she liked best. There was shrimp cocktail because someone had noticed she loved seafood. There was Lydia's special Caesar salad that Jessica had once asked for seconds on, and there was a crusty pork roast with cherry glaze because Alex thought he remembered having pork at Jessica's house as a child. There was freshly baked bread and whipped butter from a local dairy. Molly had even made a special herbal iced tea because she remembered that Jessica had once ordered it when they had eaten lunch in town.

"I can't eat another bite!" Jessica pushed her plate away and groaned. "I've never had such a feast in my life."

"You have to eat your cake," Clancy said. "I baked it."

"Devil's food," Jessica guessed, "with chocolate icing. Just like you made for the hospital picnic."

"You ate your weight in it that day," Clancy said. "We were all paying attention."

"Nothing is a secret around here." She smiled at them all. "Except this wonderful party."

"Time to open presents!" Molly jumped up and came to stand beside Jessica's chair.

"Maybe Jessica would like to rest a little while," Lydia said, her eyes filled with concern. "We may be rushing her too much."

"Not a chance." Jessica stood, too, and let Molly lead her into the living room. Everyone followed.

Alex came to sit on the sofa beside her, and Molly and Clancy flopped at her feet. Lydia presented her with the first present. "This is from Ben and me."

Jessica carefully unwrapped the big rectangular package. The moment was too special to rush through. Inside she found another box and then another. "Someone here has a sense of humor," she said with a husky laugh. Five boxes later she found a small key and a note. "Unlock me." Jessica dangled the key. "What do I do now?"

"I guess you'll have to find the lock that goes to," Lydia said innocently.

Jessica stood. "Any hints on where to look?"

"Only that it'll be in plain sight when you find the right location."

With everyone trailing her and Alex holding her hand, Jessica led them all through the house. Nothing seemed different in any other rooms, and nothing was sporting a lock. "Alex," she asked, squeezing his hand, "do you know anything about this?"

"Everything."

"And you're not going to tell me, are you?"

"Nope."

Downstairs again, Jessica stood in the hallway trying to figure out where to look next. Alex put his arm around her waist and pulled her to stand close to his side.

"I could try the garage," she said, thinking out loud.

The entire family applauded. Jessica pulled away from Alex and went to the front door. "Or I could try the attic."

Everybody booed.

Like a shot, Jessica was out the door racing toward the garage. There in front of the Bancrofts' station wagon was a bright blue three-speed bicycle decorated with ribbons and another Happy Birthday Jessica sign.

"I love it!" she said, clapping her hands. "It's perfect! Thank you, Ben. Thank you, Lydia." She gave them both a hug and then bent over and unlocked the bicycle lock. "Does anyone want to go for a ride?"

"Not yet. You've still got the rest of your presents to open," Molly reminded her.

"More?"

"Of course. Clancy and I bought you something and so did Alex."

Molly took an oddly shaped package off the utility shelf on the garage wall. "From Clancy and me."

Jessica pulled the wrapping off to discover a bike helmet and knee pads.

"So you won't kill yourself," Clancy said unnecessarily.

"You stinkers!" Jessica wrapped her arms around both of them and gave them bear hugs. "I'm assigning more scale work first thing tomorrow."

"Alex still has a present for you," Molly said, when she could talk again.

"Is your present in the garage, too?" Jessica asked him. Alex had been standing to one side watching the joyous nonsense, and now he stepped closer. Everyone else moved back as if they knew this present was just between Jessica and Alex.

"My present is in the corner." He held out his hand and Jessica took it to follow him across the garage. There, decorated with the same ribbon that had adorned the bicycle, was a gleaming pair of cross-country skis, with boots and poles to go with them. "I specialize in firsts," he said softly enough for only Jessica to hear.

"And are you going to teach me to ski?" she asked just as softly.

"It will be my privilege."

The rest of the evening proceeded in a joyous blur. With Alex's arm around her, Jessica followed the Bancroft family back into the house. Molly and Clancy had decided to provide entertainment for the evening, and everyone followed them into the music room where each gave a performance that made Jessica cry. Clancy played "Maple Leaf Rag" flawlessly from memory, following it with another Joplin tune that Jessica hadn't even assigned. He finished with his own rendition of a medley of Billy Joel's greatest hits. Molly played three Chopin Preludes and finished with the *Minute* Waltz because Lydia had told her it was the piece Jessica liked when she was happy.

Afterward Lydia and Ben served the birthday cake and everyone sang another round of "Happy Birthday."

"Speech, speech," Clancy called after Jessica had blown out the candles and cut slices for everyone.

What was there to say? How could she tell these wonderful people just what they'd come to mean to her? Did she tell them that they'd touched the lonely little girl inside her in a way that no one ever had before? And did she tell them that having Alex there had made the night perfect for her? That once again she was filled with hope that he might really be learning to love her?

"Once upon a time," she said quietly, "there was a little girl who lived in a big house with two kindly parents." The room became very still as she talked, but Jessica was so caught up in her own words that she didn't notice. "She loved her parents very much, but sometimes, when she was feeling lonely, she wished that she had a different life. She wished she lived somewhere where she could ride a bicycle and roller-skate on the sidewalk, and she wished she lived somewhere where she had a brother and a sister to play with and fight with and get dirty with. Then one day her parents died, and she realized that no matter what their faults, they had been good parents and she had been very lucky.

"The girl traveled to another land, far away, and she was taken in by a new family. They were like the family she had often dreamed about, and there, with them, she learned to be free, to have fun and to say whatever she wanted. And in that land was a handsome prince who taught her what it was like to fall in love." Jessica turned to Alex.

"The girl spent months in the new land, and when it came time for her to go, she found that she didn't want to leave at all. The new family felt like they were her own, and the handsome prince had turned into the best friend she had ever had." Jessica stopped, unable to go on.

"Jessica, sweetheart." Lydia rose and folded her arms around Jessica. "We love you, too. You're part of our family. Forever. Don't go. Stay here and make a life for yourself in Lindleton."

Lydia stepped back, and then Alex was in front of Jessica. "I want you to stay, too," he said.

Jessica was overcome with the emotion of the moment. She smiled, but her lips trembled. "No matter what I decide," she said, "I'll always love all of you. You'll never know what these months have meant to me." Alex's arms came around her and right there, in front of the whole Bancroft family, he gave her a heart-stopping kiss.

"Can we eat now?" Clancy's cheerful words broke the tension and the embrace, and wiping tears away, Jessica served the cake and joined in the easy laughter. She was very aware that Alex was beside her, his hand on her knee under the table. Although she didn't know exactly what his words or the kiss had meant, she did know that he cared about her. The night had shown her that, and for the first time she felt that the differences between them might be resolved.

"We have to have a picture for the birthday book,"

Molly said when everyone had almost finished the cake. "Mom, you never forget that."

"What's the birthday book?" Alex asked.

"Our special occasion book," Molly explained. "Only the most important pictures get put in there. Birthdays, Christmases, those kind of things. I'll get my camera." Molly ran out of the room.

"It's the very last tradition you have to put up with," Lydia assured Jessica.

"I've loved every minute of it."

A few minutes later Jessica posed as Molly snapped her photograph with a camera that developed its own film. In thirty seconds Molly was passing the picture around for everyone to admire. "Now I'm going to put it in the birthday book."

Jessica found that she couldn't sit still any longer. She was brimming over with emotion. "I want to see this special book," she said, standing to follow Molly.

In the living room she sat next to Molly on the sofa and watched her fasten Jessica's photograph to one of the pages in the album. The rest of the family came in, too, except for Lydia who could be heard banging pots and plates in the kitchen.

"Don't make Jessica sit through all those old pictures," Ben protested. "No punishment on her birthday."

Molly ignored him and began to leaf through the album, explaining each picture to Jessica. There was no apparent order to the progression of photographs. It was a hodgepodge of delightfully candid shots, and Jessica admired them all.

"These pictures are of Daddy's relatives," Molly said, turning the pages quickly. "Only important ones, though. Nobody unimportant gets in the birth-day book.''

Lydia entered the room with a tray of coffee cups. ''I got coffee for everyone.''

Jessica looked up and smiled her thanks. The look that crossed Lydia's face was peculiar, and for a moment Jessica thought Lydia was going to cry.

''Molly, Jessica doesn't want to see all those pictures,'' Lydia said. Her voice sounded upset, too.

''Don't worry,'' Jessica assured her. ''I love it.''

Molly turned the page and Jessica glanced at it. Just as Molly turned the page again, a photograph caught Jessica's eye. ''Wait.''

Molly turned back. ''That's a shot of one of my cousins, I think. Mom, who is this?''

Jessica stared at the beautifully done photograph of a little girl sitting at a table with a big birthday cake in front of her. The little girl was all big eyes and red hair and her expression was solemn. Jessica had seen the picture before. It had been on page six of her parents' neatly arranged photograph album.

Lydia came to sit on the other side of Jessica, and she covered Jessica's hand with her own. Neither woman said a word.

''What's the problem?'' Molly asked finally.

''Lydia,'' Jessica began, ''where did you get this photograph?''

''Your parents sent it to me through Alex's father.'' Lydia gripped Jessica's hand a little harder.

''Why?''

This time Lydia's voice was shaking. ''Because they were kind, concerned people who knew I needed to see that you were all right.''

For a moment Jessica felt nothing. It was as if all her previous emotions had drained away, leaving her empty. Then new feelings began to surge through her. She felt betrayed. She felt angry and hurt and terribly confused. How could she not have suspected?

Jessica tried to control her voice. The room was silent. "You've known all along, haven't you?"

Lydia nodded. "All along."

"And that explains how you knew my birth date."

"It's a day I will never forget."

Jessica shut her eyes. Her suspicions had been confirmed, and yet the truth was so shattering that she could hardly comprehend it. "So all of this was a setup," she said slowly. "You've known who I was, but you didn't trust me enough to tell me who you were."

"Jessica, what's wrong?" Molly's voice betrayed her bewilderment. "Why are you mad at my mother?"

"Your mother." Jessica swallowed hard. She could not bring herself to reveal the truth to Molly, who obviously had no more idea of their relationship than she herself had had until a few moments before. How could she tell the younger girl that Lydia was Jessica's mother, too?

"It's all right, Jessica. It's time for everyone to know," Lydia said.

"No!" Jessica stood. "Please excuse me."

"Jessica, wait!" Lydia put her hand on Jessica's arm. "Please talk to me."

"I can't." Jessica pulled away from Lydia's grasp and hurried to leave the room, but Alex stepped in her way.

Jessica faced him, her eyes blazing with anger. "You knew, didn't you?"

"Yes."

"And that's why you invited me to Lindleton."

Alex nodded.

Jessica shook her head and pushed past him.

Upstairs she began to take clothes out of her closet and put them in her suitcases. She ignored the knock on her door; she didn't even turn to see who it was when she heard the door opening.

"I can understand why you're upset." Alex put his arms around her waist and tried to pull her to lean against him. Jessica jerked away.

"Can you?" Her voice was heavy with sarcasm. "Just because I've been lied to and treated like an imbecile?"

"No one thought you were an imbecile."

"Then why didn't you tell me the truth right away?" Jessica put her hands on her hips and faced him.

"I'd like to tell you the whole story, if you'll let me."

Jessica stared at him for a moment, and then she shrugged her shoulders. "You can tell me while I pack."

Alex sat on the bed and watched her fold clothes and drop them in her suitcase. "I'd been in Lindleton for about three months when Lydia approached me. I'd met her at a couple of parties, and I knew Ben fairly well by then. Lydia came to my office one day to talk to me. She told me that she'd known a Dr. Grainger in Pittsburgh, and she wanted to know if he was any relation."

"Convenient." Jessica threw an armful of lingerie in the suitcase.

Alex went on. "I told her that he was my father, but that he had died several years before. Lydia confessed that my father had delivered her first baby, a little girl that she had named Jessica, and that two years later, when she could no longer care for the child, she had asked my father to arrange an adoption."

"And that's when you should have come to me!"

Alex's voice was soothing. "Jessie, I couldn't. Your parents were dying; you had too many other things to worry about. I told Lydia that I knew where you were. You have no idea how grateful she was. She'd been trying to trace you for years, but because my father had died and the court records were sealed, she had no way of finding out where you were. She had given up hope of ever locating you."

"She could have put her name on an adoption registry."

"She did. *You* didn't."

Jessica nodded. That much was true.

Alex continued. "Lydia begged me to arrange a meeting. I was reluctant to expose you to more emotional upheaval, but when your parents died, Lydia insisted that you needed her. I knew how lost you must be feeling, and I knew the Bancrofts would be good for you. I made Lydia promise that she wouldn't reveal her identity until I thought the time was right."

"When was the time going to be right, Alex?" Jessica snapped her last suitcase shut. "When I finally grew up enough to hear the truth?"

He was silent.

"It's funny, really," she continued. "You thought I was enough of an adult to share your bed, but not enough of one to know the truth about my own mother." She cocked her head and examined him. "I wonder if this will teach you a lesson. You've always put women in one of two roles. Either they're objects of your desire, or children you need to protect."

"I can understand your anger."

"I couldn't care less if you understand my anger." Jessica set the suitcase on the floor. "But there is something I hope you do understand. Trust and the sharing of feelings are the most important things that can happen between a man and a woman. The rest is so much icing on the cake. And until you do understand that, you'll never have a satisfactory relationship with anyone."

Alex stood. "Leaving like this won't solve a thing."

"Stop taking care of me!"

He smoothed her hair back from her face, and ran his thumbs along her cheekbones. "What if I ask you to stay?"

"Why?"

"Because I want you to."

"And Alex always gets what he wants." Jessica stepped away from him. "Not this time." She turned and picked up her suitcases.

"You at least owe Lydia more than an empty farewell."

"Thank you Dr. Grainger, but I think I can manage my relationship with Lydia without your help from now on." At the door she turned. "Goodbye. It's been an education."

Alex had no reply.

Downstairs Jessica deposited her suitcases beside the front door. She was trying to decide what to do about saying goodbye to Molly and Clancy when Lydia came into the hall.

"I have to go somewhere and sort this out," Jessica said bluntly. "I feel like my whole life has been turned upside down."

"Please come back when you're ready." A tear ran slowly down Lydia's cheek.

Jessica nodded and turned to go.

"Jessica?"

Jessica stopped with her hand on the doorknob. "Yes?"

"Please know that I never stopped loving you. Not when I had to give you up, not all those years when I couldn't be with you. Everything else may seem topsy-turvy, but that will never change."

With a small sob, Jessica opened the door, picked up her suitcases and started down the path to the driveway.

Chapter Ten

Jessica parked across the street from the house where she had grown up in Shadyside, one of Pittsburgh's more gracious neighborhoods, and waited for the dark green Oldsmobile in the driveway to pull out into traffic. She glimpsed an older man and woman in the car along with the driver, Carl Perkins, who was Jessica's real estate agent. Carl had called her earlier that morning and specifically requested that she not be present when he brought the couple to see the house. It was their third visit, and Carl was sure that he would be presenting Jessica with a good offer that evening.

Jessica had always been awed by the neighborhood of old houses in the architectural style that someone had cheerfully dubbed "Gilded Age High-Ceilinged." Her parents' house fitted the description, and although it was a wonderful house, Jessica had found it intimidating as a young child to be surrounded by so much splendor. Now she was torn between being relieved and sad that it would soon be sold. The house was her last link with her parents and with the life she had previously led.

The green Oldsmobile had been gone for minutes before she pulled her car into the driveway and parked it. Every time she entered the house she was overwhelmed by the silence that greeted her. She had dismissed her parents' staff before she had gone to Lindleton, and now there was only a cleaning lady who came twice a week to dust and polish antiques. Jessica had not announced her return, avoiding the places where she could expect to see people that she knew. The only conversations she had were with Mr. Perkins.

She unlocked the front door and stepped inside. She had opened all the curtains and set fresh flowers on the mahogany table in the hall, just as Mr. Perkins had asked her to do. The interior looked somber and formal except for the flowers and an occasional sunbeam that broke through the dense cloud cover of the September afternoon. The house needed people who would love it as her parents had.

Jessica stood in the hallway, wondering how she should spend the rest of the day. In the three weeks that she had been back in Pittsburgh she had organized herself for her coming move. She had tagged furniture that she wanted to keep and taken offers from antique dealers on everything she didn't. She had packed away mementos and memories and readied herself for her new life. The only thing she hadn't done was to make a decision about where she was going to go after the house was sold. Now she realized that she could no longer put off that decision.

Her thoughts were interrupted by the chiming of the front door bell. The sound was startling. She realized the extent of her loneliness by her reaction to it. Even if her caller was a door-to-door salesman, she would be glad to talk to him.

Jessica opened the door and caught the movement of a taxi pulling away from the curb. More interesting, however, was her visitor.

"Molly! What are you doing here?" Jessica impulsively opened her arms, and Molly came into them for a hug.

"Would you believe me if I said I was just passing by?"

Jessica felt tears flood her eyes, and she hugged Molly harder. Suddenly, she didn't feel alone anymore. "Come in," she said, when she felt it was safe to talk again.

Inside, Jessica examined Molly. "How did you get here, other than the taxi?"

"I took the bus."

"By yourself?"

Molly nodded.

Jessica tried to decipher the guilty expression on Molly's face. Suddenly she understood. "You didn't tell anyone you were coming, did you?"

Molly shook her head.

"Oh, Molly." Jessica shook her head, too, and started toward the kitchen. "Let me get you something to drink and then we'll talk."

A few minutes later they were settled on a love seat in the solarium. It had always been Jessica's favorite room, light and airy and easy to be a child in. Now it was the perfect place to bring Molly. "It's time to tell me why you're here," Jessica said with no preliminaries. "And then you've got to call your mother and tell her where you are. She must be sick with worry."

Molly looked at her watch. "I doubt if she even knows I'm gone. I went to the bus station instead of school this morning. Unless the dean of students called her, she thinks I'm just finishing up sixth period."

"And if he called?" Jessica asked, one eyebrow raised.

"Then she'll be frantic," Molly conceded.

"Why did you come?"

Molly toyed with the glass of iced tea that Jessica had poured for her. She was obviously trying to think of the right way to put her feelings into words. Finally her eyes found Jessica's. "I wanted to find out if you were angry at me."

Jessica was instantly ashamed. She had been so caught up in her own emotions that she had not given Molly or Clancy more than a passing thought. She had been so busy reconciling her new relationship to them that she had ignored what they might be feeling. She bent and put her hand on Molly's knee. "Of course I'm not angry with you. You've done nothing to upset me. Nothing in the world."

"But you left so suddenly."

"I know I did. But that had nothing to do with you and Clancy."

"Well, that's not exactly true." Molly leaned back

against the cushions and regarded Jessica. "It had a lot to do with me, actually."

Jessica waited.

"I know I'm your sister," Molly said finally.

Jessica felt herself relax. She hadn't known if Molly had been told the story. "Does Clancy know?"

"Yes."

"How do you both feel about it?"

"It took a while to get over the shock." Molly was frowning. "It wasn't that we weren't glad to have you as a real sister, it was just that everything fell into place so suddenly that it was hard to absorb it."

Jessica nodded. "And now?" she asked softly.

"Now we're just confused."

"About what?"

"About why you left, and why you're mad at Mom."

Jessica searched for the right way to explain her actions. "It was more of a shock for me than anyone, Molly. I'd grown to love all of you, but I had no idea that Lydia was…is my mother. I felt…feel as though I was lied to, and I felt like a fool for not realizing the truth."

"I don't see how any of us missed it," Molly said. "You and I stood at the mirror and talked about how similar our faces were, but neither of us even imagined we could really be related."

"If you're not looking for answers, you seldom find them." Jessica shook her head. "It just never occurred to either of us that my invitation to come to Lindleton was anything more than a simple opportunity to teach piano for the summer."

"I can understand why you were confused and upset at first," Molly said, changing the thrust of the conversation. "But what I can't understand is why you've stayed away since you had time to think about it."

How could she talk about feelings that she didn't understand herself? Jessica tried to think of a way to put her emotions into words. She wasn't obligated to explain anything to Molly, and yet she felt a strong bond with this girl who was indeed the sister she had always wanted.

"I feel betrayed," Jessica began. "If Lydia had come to me and told me who she was, I'd have been able to accept her. As it is, I grew to love her, to love all of you, without knowing your real identities. I can't forgive your mother...Lydia...for not caring enough about my feelings to be honest with me right from the beginning."

Molly set her tea on a glass-topped coffee table and turned so that she was facing Jessica. "I think you're being pretty selfish," she stated flatly.

It was the first time Jessica had ever heard the pretty teenager lose her temper, and for a moment she was so surprised she couldn't say a thing. "Why?" she asked finally.

"Because you're thinking about yourself and not about what Mom is going through, has gone through, since she was forced to give you up for adoption."

Jessica nodded. "That's true, Molly. But frankly, my own feelings have been all I could possibly handle."

Her confession seemed to defuse Molly's anger. "I can understand that, I guess," she said. "But now it's time to start thinking about Mom."

"What am I supposed to think?"

Molly tucked her feet beneath her as if she were getting ready for a long discussion and wanted to be comfortable. "How much do you know about your own history?"

"Not as much as you do, obviously." Jessica settled back against the cushions and waited.

"I'd like to tell you the story, if you'll let me."

Molly's voice was so mature, so concerned that for a moment Jessica felt like the younger sister. She thought about the irony of having the girl who had recently been her piano student acquaint her with the story of her own life. And yet it was a story Jessica was curious about. There were many unanswered questions. She nodded, and Molly began.

"Mom was seventeen when she found out she was pregnant. The boy, your father, was also seventeen, and Mom says that although he was really a good boy at heart, he was sure that being saddled with a wife and a child would ruin his life."

"He was probably right."

Molly shrugged. "That's what Mom said, too. Anyway, he refused to marry Mom, even when her father threatened him. His parents were fairly prominent, and they protected their son. Eventually they footed the bill to send Mom to Pittsburgh to live in a rooming house, have her baby and give it up for adoption. Mom's parents told her that she didn't have any choice in the matter. When she got to Pittsburgh, though, she refused to sign the adoption papers and after she had you, she still refused to sign them.

"My grandparents—" Molly paused "—our grandparents," she amended, "were furious that

Mom wanted to keep you. They had tried very hard along with your father's parents to keep the whole thing a secret. Mom wanted to go back to Ohio..."

"She was from Ohio?" Jessica broke in.

Molly nodded. "Uh-huh. Youngstown. Fourth generation. Anyway, she wanted to go back and raise you there with their help. They refused and when she still wouldn't sign the papers, they cut off all her money to force her to do what they wanted."

Jessica felt such a surge of pity for Lydia that she couldn't speak.

Molly went on. "By then Mom had turned eighteen. She got a job as a waitress, and the lady who ran the rooming house kept you during the evenings when she was working."

"And that went on for two years?"

Molly nodded. "She managed without any help at all from anyone except the old lady who kept you. Then the old lady died, and Mom had to find another place to live. All she could afford was a room in a bad neighborhood, but the worst part was that she couldn't find anyone good to stay with you while she worked." Molly was now close to tears.

"She came home one night and found that the lady who was supposed to be staying with you wasn't there. The door was ajar, and it was only a miracle that you were all right. Mom said it was the final straw. She realized that she was never going to be able to give you the life you deserved, that without an education she was never going to be able to do any better. So she decided that the only chance for you to have a safe, happy life was if she gave you up for adoption."

"What about her parents?"

"They still wouldn't help. You know the rest of the story."

"Not quite." Jessica was so caught up in Lydia's struggle that she had to know more. "Did Lydia go back to Ohio?"

Molly shook her head. "No, she's never been back. Neither Clancy nor I have seen our grandparents, although we never knew why. Mom stayed in Pittsburgh and finished school. Eventually she even put herself through two years of college. Then she met Daddy, who was in the last year of his residency, and married him a year later."

"She deserved a happy ending," Jessica said softly.

"It wasn't a happy ending!" Molly's anger was revealed in her voice. "Don't you see? She went through hell to keep you. She loved you more than she loved her parents, more than she loved her own—" Molly fumbled for the right word "—her own security. When she had to give you up it tore her to pieces. She told me that she had nightmares for years about someone mistreating you. She's never felt she did the right thing; she's missed you terribly."

Molly's anger was Jessica's undoing. She could feel tears wet her cheeks.

Molly's voice softened. "Can't you forgive her for being afraid that she'd lose you again if she told you the truth about who she was?"

For the first time Jessica could see that there was nothing to forgive. Lydia had always done the very best she could to protect her elder daughter. Lydia had loved her enough to give her up. Lydia had loved her enough to keep her own identity a secret when she must have ached all summer to tell Jessica that Jessica was her daughter.

"Quite a woman, our mother," Jessica whispered, wiping away the tears that kept spilling down her cheeks.

"Quite a woman, my sister," Molly said, moving closer to Jessica and shyly patting her on the knee. "And now I think it's time for us to be quite a family."

Each mile that brought her closer to Lindleton made Jessica more aware of how much she had missed the little town. No, that wasn't quite true. It wasn't the town she had missed; it was the Bancroft family...and the man she loved.

"Have you seen Alex since I left?" she asked Molly, who was sitting next to her on the front seat of Jessica's car.

"No. I heard Dad tell Mom that Alex isn't around much."

"I wonder what he was talking about." Either Ben meant that Alex was working too hard and was never available for socializing, or Alex was hardly working and wasn't even available at the hospital. The statement was perplexing.

"Do you love Alex?" Molly's voice, which had recently sounded so mature, was filled once again with adolescent romanticism.

"Yes, fool that I am."

"Why do you say that?"

"Because he's the worst kind of man to love: the kind who can't take a woman seriously." Jessica had to remind herself not to take her frustration out on the gas pedal, and she slowed the car down to the speed limit.

"Gee, Jessica, it seems like you might be serious enough for both of you."

Jessica thought about Molly's words as she covered the final fifty miles to Lindleton. She had once thought that she could change Alex. She had believed that someday he would see that good times weren't enough and that a serious relationship could fill the empty places in his life. She had hoped that he would come to love her not as a sister, not as a temporary solution to his physical needs, but as a partner, a soul mate.

Perhaps she had been wrong. She had made demands on him, demands he was not able to meet. She had insisted that he change for her. Real love was acceptance, and she had never accepted Alex. She had bartered with her body, with her love, insisting that he become something he was not. Did she love Alex or did she love the image of Alex as she wanted him to be?

"Jessica?"

Jessica realized that she had just missed the turnoff to the Bancroft house. She slowed and continued down the road until she could make a U-turn. "I guess I'm nervous," she admitted to Molly.

"You don't have to be. When I called Mom she was thrilled you were going to drive me home. Everyone wants you to come back. Even Daddy says that he thinks of you as his daughter. I heard him tell Mom that if you didn't come to your senses, he was going to go down to Pittsburgh and drag you home himself.''

Despite her fears, Jessica giggled at the gentle Ben Bancroft doing anything so Neanderthal.

The granite house looked the same as Jessica pulled into the driveway. Soon the beautiful old trees surrounding the house would begin to turn colors, and summer would be a memory.

'' 'To every thing there is a season, and a time for every purpose under the heaven,''' Jessica quoted. "I've never realized what that meant before.''

"Mom's waiting for you on the porch," Molly said, squeezing Jessica's hand. "Give me a head start. I want to leave you alone with her.'' Molly opened the door and slid out.

Jessica waited. She realized that she didn't know what to say to Lydia. She hoped that when she faced the woman who had given birth to her she'd be able to find the right words to explain her feelings. Finally she could put off the moment no longer. She closed the car door behind her and began her walk through the trees and up the path.

At the porch steps she shook her hair behind her shoulders and looked up at Lydia, who was standing quietly watching her. Suddenly Jessica was reluctant to continue until she was sure that she was welcome.

"I've hoped every day that you'd come back," Lydia said softly. "I'm just sorry it had to be under these circumstances.''

Reassured, Jessica climbed the steps. "I'm not sorry," she said. "Sometimes it takes a shove from behind to get going in the right direction.''

Lydia motioned to the wicker chairs. "Will you sit and talk with me for a while?"

Jessica nodded, and they settled themselves side by side.

"You must have been surprised when Molly showed up at your front door." Lydia was looking straight ahead, and it gave Jessica a chance to examine her profile. Why hadn't she seen how much she resembled this woman? Molly resembled their mother more than Jessica did, but the similarities between Jessica and Lydia were still strong.

"Since no one else in the family has red hair, I'm assuming I got it from my father," Jessica said.

Lydia smiled and turned her chair to face Jessica's. "You did. His was a brighter red, though, and he had millions of freckles."

"May I ask what happened to him?"

"After I found you, I traced him to California. I thought he deserved to know you if he wanted to."

Jessica shrugged. "After the way you were treated I'm surprised you'd care about his rights."

"Molly told you the story?"

Jessica nodded.

"Don't forget he was barely seventeen. He was a pawn of his parents and their values."

"Have you contacted him?"

Lydia reached into the pocket of her slacks and pulled out a letter. "He's written you. He's married with three children, but in his letter to me he says he's often wondered where you were and how you turned out. Perhaps someday you can meet him."

Jessica put the letter in her purse to read at another time. "Are my grandparents still living?"

"Both sets. But, Jessica, they're of another generation. Think twice before you contact them."

"Do your parents know you found me?"

Lydia shook her head. "I haven't spoken to them since the day I realized I had to give you up."

"Is that the way they want it?"

"There are some things too terrible to forgive, Jessica."

Jessica knew that Lydia was talking about her own inability to forgive, not her parents'. "Someday," Jessica said slowly, "someday I hope you'll be able to accept what they did. They lost a daughter, too. Perhaps they deserve to find her again."

"Did I deserve to find my daughter?" Lydia put her hand on the arm of Jessica's chair. "Should I have stayed out of your life forever? Have I been unfair to you?"

"I can't help wishing that it had all happened a little differently," Jessica answered. "But, no, I'm glad you've found me, that we've found each other." She covered Lydia's hand with her own. "I've always wondered, deep inside, why my birth mother gave me away. I've always felt that there must have been something wrong with me, that somehow I was a disappointment..."

Lydia's hand tightened convulsively. "There was nothing wrong with you! You were perfect. I adored you."

"I know that now. And I feel different, knowing it. And I feel different knowing that you've cared enough all these years to try and find me. I never want to lose you again."

They linked fingers and both women swallowed

tears. "I know you'll never think of me as your mother," Lydia said, "but I hope there'll be a special place in your life for me, because you hold a very special place in mine."

Jessica thought about Lydia's words, and she heard the pain of Lydia's loss behind them. "Look," she said, trying not to cry, "you have two daughters, and I know that you don't love either of us less because of it."

Lydia nodded her head.

"Well, I have two mothers," Jessica continued, her eyes dropping to their linked fingers. "My love for one doesn't diminish my love for the other."

"Thank you," Lydia said, tears in her voice. "You don't know what that means to me."

"I think I do," Jessica lifted her eyes to Lydia's. "You and I have shared twenty years of missing each other."

Lydia smiled a watery smile. "I hope from now on we can share more than that. Will you stay in Lindleton for a while?"

Jessica squeezed her hand. "Yes, I'll stay. I hear there's an opening for a piano teacher in town."

"And for a daughter," Lydia said, standing to open her arms.

"Looks like I've got my work cut out for me." Jessica stood up to embrace Lydia. "But I think I'm up to both jobs."

Chapter Eleven

Jessica found that she was painlessly reabsorbed into the Bancroft family as soon as she stepped over the threshold. Clancy, with a teasing grin, told her that he couldn't imagine anything worse than another sister; Molly held the telephone away from her ear to ask if Jessica would consider giving Mike piano lessons; Ben welcomed her with a fatherly hug. Dinner was relaxed and happy, with everyone catching Jessica up on Lindleton gossip. The only name she didn't hear mentioned throughout the festive meal was Alex's.

After dinner Jessica joined Lydia and Ben on the porch while Clancy and Molly cleaned the kitchen. There was a chilly breeze blowing, heralding a coming storm, and Lydia went inside to get sweaters for them. Jessica waited with Ben, anxious to ask about Alex and simultaneously afraid of what she might find. It was Ben, finally, who brought up the subject.

"Have you been in touch with Alex?" he asked.

Jessica was ashamed that she couldn't answer yes. "No, we had a fight before I left Lindleton. I haven't heard from him since."

"I've hardly seen him myself."

"Why is that? Isn't he around the hospital?"

"Not as much as usual. His partner seems to be pulling his own weight for a change."

Jessica was intrigued by Ben's answer. "What do you mean?"

"Well, Alex's partner, Tom Starke, is an excellent physician and a hard worker, but after a few months of Alex's obsessive schedule, Tom began to back off."

"I don't understand."

Ben explained. "Tom was willing to split the work fifty-fifty, but Alex kept doing more than his share. Alex doesn't know how to say no; he doesn't know how to pace himself. Eventually, rather than continually confront Alex, I think Tom just stepped back and let Alex assume the greater amount of responsibility."

"So Alex doesn't have to work as hard as he does?"

"No, he doesn't. There are enough doctors in town for Alex and Tom to limit their practice, but Alex still insists on accepting every new patient that walks through the door."

"Why?" Jessica couldn't understand why Alex, who loved the good life, would be so overly conscientious.

"I don't know. I thought maybe you had some insight into it."

Jessica shrugged. "None at all."

Lydia returned with a sweater for Ben and one of her own for Jessica. "I couldn't help overhearing," she said as she draped the sweater around Jessica's shoulders. "I have a hunch about why Alex works so hard."

Ben took his sweater and pulled Lydia down to sit beside him in the wide wicker chair. "Why?" he asked her.

"I think he's acting like his father."

Jessica considered Lydia's words, but before she could respond, Lydia continued.

"I only knew the senior Dr. Grainger as a patient, but if he was half as available to the rest of his patients as he was to me, he never must have been at home."

"That's close to the truth," Jessica said, thinking about the man who had been such a good friend of her parents. "I remember my mother saying once that the reason Alex was an only child was because his father was too busy running all over town delivering babies to make another one of his own."

"If that's true, it must have put an awful strain on the Graingers' marriage," Lydia said.

Jessica thought about the conversation after Lydia and Ben had gone inside to get Molly and Clancy started on their homework. The night was dark with no stars, and the trees rustled briskly. A wave of loneliness swept through her. She had thought her reunion with Lydia and the Bancroft family would fill the empty place inside her, but now Jessica realized that she had been lying to herself.

A huge part of her past was resolved. But a huge part of her future was not. Yes, she had decided to move to Lindleton, to put down roots near her new family, but no, she had not made any decisions about the man she loved. Loving her family and being reconciled with them was not enough. The time had come to find Alex and settle their relationship once and for all.

She had spent three weeks ignoring her feelings, and now they blossomed forth in glory. She loved Alex. She loved him, but still, from the beginning, she had tried to change him. Instead he needed unqualified acceptance as the man he really was. He was not just a good time man, he was a man who could cry over a tiny baby's death and a man who could offer protection and support to an old friend. She had never given him that acceptance, nor had he ever accepted the real Jessica Cassidy. Now they must see each other without the blinders of the past, without secrets, and find out if love had a chance to succeed.

"Jessica, are you coming inside?" Lydia stood in the doorway with a concerned expression on her face.

"Lydia, I've got something I have to do. I'll be gone for a while."

Lydia nodded, but her expression was still concerned. "Good luck," she said softly. "No matter what, Alex is worth whatever trouble he gives you."

"I finally realized that," Jessica said. "And that's exactly what I'm going to tell him."

* * *

The trees lining the long driveway to Alex's house were bending and swaying in the wind that seemed to increase by the second. Jessica shivered, as much in anticipation of the harsh winter to come as from a real chill.

Winter in northwestern Pennsylvania would best be spent in the arms of a lover. For a moment she allowed herself to imagine Alex in front of his fireplace, a blanket of snow on the ground outside. She imagined herself beside him, feeding him roasted chestnuts, snuggling into his arms. He would kiss her, the fire would die down for lack of attention, and finally...they would fall asleep together in front of the glowing embers.

Jessica parked the car in front of the house and admired its stark lines against the clouded night sky. Somehow the house was much like Alex's life. It was a house designed for good times, and yet it was isolated and empty except for brief periods. It was silent, lonely. The house called out to be filled with warmth and with love. Jessica only hoped that someday Alex would understand that, too.

Knocking on the door leading into Alex's garage was not appealing. She couldn't imagine standing stiffly beside his Porsche to exchange greetings. Instead she walked around the side of the house and on to the deck that led inside to his hot tub. There was a lamp lit in the middle of the room and, as she tapped on the glass door, she searched for him.

At first there appeared to be no one at home, then as Jessica watched, Alex's head appeared over the back of the sofa. Evidently she had caught him in the middle of a nap. Her eyes widened as she realized that she could have caught him doing more. There she stood, staring into the room that had been designed for an eligible bachelor, and she hadn't even thought that if Alex was there he might not be alone.

He stood and turned, pushing his hair off his forehead in a sleepy gesture. Jessica stepped back and waited for him, but for a long moment he didn't move. Finally he made his way across the room and slid the door open.

It was too windy outside to worry about hasty entrances. Jessica stepped into the room and gave a grateful sigh. "It's cold out there," she murmured, rubbing her arms in a gesture that had more to do with apprehension than with restoring lost warmth.

"So you came back." There was no trace of the Alex she knew in the voice that answered her. He was as cold as the wind whipping through the trees, as cold as the rain that was no longer threatening but was beginning to pelt the deck behind them.

"It looks like I got here just in time," she said, wondering why she was making small talk. "It sounds like that's going to be quite a storm."

"If you came to give me a weather report, Jessie, I could have saved you a trip. I have a television and I always watch the eleven o'clock news."

"I came to give you a Jessie and Alex report," she said, hurt by his words but determined to continue, anyway.

"I don't think I'm interested."

Jessica had never heard Alex be rude to anyone.

Now she was taken aback by the venom in his tone. The storm seemed a safer alternative than staying inside to face his anger.

As if he had read her thoughts, Alex turned and stomped to the fireplace. "You can't go back outside," he grumbled. "You'll have to stay until the rain stops." He crumpled newspaper and took kindling out of a copper washtub on the hearth. In a moment a small fire was blazing. Alex waited until the kindling caught before he added several logs.

Jessica stood by the door and watched the whole ritual. There was anger in every move Alex made. But watching him bend and stir the fire with a cast iron poker, Jessica began to realize just how positive his anger was. Once she had wondered if he felt any deep emotions. Since then she had learned that he could feel great sadness, and she had learned that he could feel protective. But she had not known that he could become so angry. Only someone who mattered very much to him could infuriate him this way.

She tested her theory. "I've never seen you this mad."

"I've never been this mad."

"Are you going to tell me about it, or are you going to stomp around the room until the rain stops?"

"Don't try to be cute, Jessie. I'm not in the mood." He bent again and repositioned a log that didn't need repositioning.

"What mood are you in, then?" Tentatively she moved a little closer to the fire, which was now beginning to give off welcome heat.

"If I told you, you'd find something wrong with it," he muttered.

She considered his answer. "I promise I wouldn't." She moved a little closer, but she stepped back when he straightened and turned.

"Then that would be a first!"

The glow from the fire set off the golden highlights in his hair and mustache. He had lost some of his tan, but his green eyes still provided emphasis for a face that really didn't need it at all. Tonight she noticed an increased number of tiny lines around his eyes. He looked tired, almost haggard, and she was overwhelmed with guilt.

"Alex, have you been taking care of yourself?" she asked softly.

His smile was made up equally of anger and triumph. "Let's see if I can paraphrase a speech you once gave me." He smiled again and this time the smile was pure ice. "You seem to put men in one of two roles, Jessie. Either they're objects you desire, or children you need to take care of. Until you understand that trust and sharing of feelings are the most important things that can happen between a man and a woman, you'll never have a satisfactory relationship with anyone." He paused for effect. "Did I get it right?"

"You left out the part about the icing on the cake." Jessica stepped closer to the fire and wondered if the heat she felt was from the burning logs or from Alex's temper.

"Why are you here, Jessie?"

"To apologize. To admit I've been a self-righteous

prig and ask you to forgive me." She gave him a tentative smile that was more like a plea.

"Why? Do you need absolution? Fine. I hereby absolve the perfect Miss Jessica Cassidy from whatever minor sins she's committed in her twenty-three years." He turned back to the fire and thrust his hands in his pockets.

"I don't need absolution, Alex. I need you."

"On whose terms?"

It was a question for which she didn't have an answer. She was still the unsophisticated Jessica who knew she couldn't handle a short-term affair. He was still the sophisticated Alex who had handled many. She had told Alex that love was trust and sharing. Now it was her job to share her feelings with him and trust that he wouldn't hurt her. That was the only chance they had.

"Before we talk about terms, I want to tell you how I feel."

"I feel another lecture coming on."

Jessie held out her hand to him. "Please?"

She was beginning to wonder if she could hold her hand aloft any longer when he finally took it. He pulled her beside him and then dropped her hand. "Wait here," he said gruffly.

He returned in a minute with two large cushions, placing them on the high brick hearth. Alex settled himself on one, and motioned for her to join him. Jessica sat, too, and locked her hands around her knees.

"Are you in the mood for another first?" she asked him when the silence got to be too much to bear.

"I doubt it."

"Will you humor me?"

He didn't answer, and Jessica took it as a sign that he would listen. "I've been wrong, Alex," she began. "I pretended that I loved you, when what I loved was the man I wanted you to be. The funny thing is that I've discovered that you really are that man, but I didn't trust you enough all along to recognize it."

"That sounds like so much double-talk."

Jessica winced, but she brightened when she realized that his tone had softened. She tried again. "What I'm trying to say is that I've been insisting that you change when all along you've been exactly the man I wanted. I've been the one who hasn't trusted, not you. I still think you were wrong not to tell me about Lydia, but I know you did it because you thought it was best for me. You cared enough about me to risk my anger if I discovered the truth."

"When I made the decision," he said, "I hadn't seen you in years. In my mind you were still an immature teenager. When you came to Lindleton, I realized my mistake, but by then you'd already fitted yourself into the Bancroft family and..." His voice trailed off.

"And what?" Jessica turned a little, and her knees brushed his.

"And you'd fitted yourself into my life. I didn't want to jeopardize that." Alex moved away and leaned against the corner of the fireplace to watch the flames.

Jessica squeezed her eyes shut to force back the tears that wanted to escape. "On my birthday," she said, struggling with each word, "you told me that you'd teach me to ski. Was that your way of letting me know you wanted me to stay in Lindleton? That you wanted me in your life?"

"I suppose it was."

"And I spoiled it." Jessica turned from him to wipe away the tears that had finally won their freedom.

"It was my fault, too."

She nodded. "Yes, it was. But I'm more to blame than you are."

"We've both made a mess of things." Alex still made no move to touch her.

"Is it too late to try again?" Jessica faced him. "I've decided to move to Lindleton and buy a house."

"Is that contingent on my answer?"

"No. I want to be near my family. I love them, I love Lindleton—" she paused, and then plunged ahead "—and I love you. No matter what you say now, Alex, I'm going to stay around."

He reached for her then, dragging her across the smooth brick hearth to lie against his chest. "Why?" he asked harshly. "Do you still have some adolescent fantasy about making me into the kind of man you want?"

"You are the man I want." Jessica's hand trembled but she smoothed it across his cheeks, trying to soften the angry lines. "I don't want to change you."

"No?" His mouth sought hers, and she felt her own give way under his onslaught. This was no gentle lover, this was a man with needs that had reached a near volcanic force. His hands were making simultaneous demands, molding the hills and valleys of her body with educated determination.

Jessica relaxed against him, allowing herself to be pulled into the whirlpool of sensuality. He was still furious, still trying to prove something incomprehensible to her, but Jessica knew that Alex would never hurt her. Alex would never push her further than she wanted to go.

He lifted her to lie on top of him. Jessica shook her hair around them, an auburn cape that outshone the flames at their side. She bent her head to find his mouth again, but he denied her access to it, turning his head. Instead she kissed his cheek, his ear, the side of his nose, the corner of his mouth. She whispered apologies to him, stroking his hair and kissing his forehead. She told him again that she loved him, that she always would.

Jessica could feel the anger leave him. His body became less rigid, his arms tightened around her. He turned his head and found her mouth and this time the kiss was gentler, if no less thorough. When his hands began to travel, to circle her waist, to cup her bottom, it was hunger and not anger that seemed to possess him. Finally he rolled over, bringing her to lie beside him on the edge of the hearth.

"What happens, Jessie, if I tell you that I'm still the same old good time man you once accused me of being?"

His eyes were the mysterious green of an unexplored forest. She must venture ahead, hoping that the new discoveries she'd make would be worth the risks.

"Why have you always worked so hard to give people that impression?" she asked, her hand on his cheek. "You even fooled me for a while."

"What if it's true?"

"But it isn't," she said. Assurance that she was right marked every syllable.

Alex closed his eyes and for a moment, he resembled a man who has fought a long and mighty battle. And lost. "It's so much easier if no one knows how I really feel," he said finally.

"Why?" She stroked his cheek and his forehead, desperate to bring him some relief from whatever problem he struggled with.

"Because then there's no risk of getting hurt. That's why I've never wanted to share myself."

Jessica frowned, and Alex opened his eyes. He bent and kissed away the furrows in her brow. "Not until you came back into my life, anyway."

Jessica suspected that his answer was important, but it was also incomprehensible. She sat up and took his hand. Silently she led him to the wide sofa where he had been sleeping before she had arrived. She lay down and held out her arms, and he lay down facing her.

"You're afraid of getting hurt?" she asked. "That's why you've never wanted a serious relationship?"

"Jessie, I decided a long time ago that I would never drag a woman through the hell of being a doctor's wife. I watched my own parents fight about my father's job every day of my life until I went away to school. Our house was a living nightmare."

"I never knew." Jessica put one arm over Alex's side and drew him closer. "I always thought your parents were terrific."

"They were terrific at hiding what was going on at home." Alex wound a long strand of Jessica's hair around his hand. "My mother would demand that my father find more time for us, then my father would get angry and find more excuses to stay away. The cycle went on, exactly like that, until my father died. At one time they may have been very much in love, but any positive feelings eventually died under the strain of Dad's career."

"And so when you decided to become a doctor, you also decided that you couldn't have a serious relationship with a woman because the same thing would happen."

"It wasn't that automatic or that well thought out. I never said those words to myself." Jessica could tell that Alex was phrasing his explanation carefully, as if it was important that she understand. She waited for him to continue. "I just know that every time I began to get close to a woman, I'd feel trapped. Eventually I just chose women I wouldn't have to worry about."

Jessica wanted to ask him if he'd changed, if he would now consider a commitment. But the question would be asked from distrust. If she really believed Alex, she would also believe that having gone this far, he would also, eventually, go further. "I must have scared you to death," she said instead. "I was so adamant about wanting a real relationship with you."

"Are you apologizing?" His voice was tender, and he moved closer so that for a moment his lips were buried in her hair. "You don't need to, Jessie. If it hadn't been for you, I might never have understood what was driving me."

She could feel every part of him against her, and for a moment, she couldn't concentrate on his words. Longing shot through her. She wanted to spend all the winters of her life wrapped in Alex's arms. She wanted the barriers between them to disappear immediately so that they could concentrate on being together rather than on what was keeping them apart.

"I love you," she said against the slight roughness of his cheek. "I love you enough to take you on your terms, Alex. Whatever they are."

"And you think, don't you, that eventually I'll love you, too? That eventually I'll want our relationship to become permanent?" Alex moved back slightly so that their eyes were only inches apart. "Be honest, Jessie. You're saying you'll become my lover, but you're really gambling on marriage."

Jessica nodded her head. "I am."

"You think that instead of growing tired of you, I'll grow to love you. That instead of growing away from each other, we'll grow together. That instead of feeling trapped, I'll feel that I've finally been given my freedom."

She couldn't have said it better herself. Jessica nodded again. "I do."

Alex shook his head. "Well, you're wrong."

She smiled. His words had been said with such

warmth that she knew there was more to come. "Am I?"

This time he nodded. "All those things have already happened."

For a full minute, she couldn't absorb his meaning. Then she understood. "You love me?"

"I do."

"You want more than an affair?"

"I want to marry you."

Jessica's forehead crinkled in a frown. "Are you sure?"

Alex exploded with laughter, and the last inch between them disappeared as he pulled her tightly against him. "I'm sure," he promised. "Absolutely."

"But you were so angry with me a little while ago." She still couldn't put it in perspective. She only knew that her head was spinning from his proposal, and her body was spinning from his close proximity.

"I was furious. I thought that I'd lost you after I'd finally found you."

"When did you find me?"

He kissed her hair. "I did some serious soul-searching after the day of the baby's funeral. I realized that I'd never let anyone get close to me, but somehow you'd managed to wear away my defenses. At first it scared me to death; I didn't want to let you get close again. Then I started to understand why I was scared. By the day of your birthday party, I finally understood what had been driving me. I'd worked like a maniac for two weeks, but the work hadn't even begun to touch the pain inside me. I realized, finally, that loving you was the only way I was ever going to be whole.''

Jessica wanted to cry. "You loved me? The night of my birthday when I said all those terrible things to you?''

"I'd just realized it.''

"And I ruined it!''

"Does this feel like anything's been ruined?'' He turned her face to his and began to place rows of tiny kisses on her forehead.

"It did when I walked in the door.''

"I was hurt. And I guess I didn't trust you enough to believe that you'd be able to see you'd made a mistake, too.''

Jessica realized from his words just how vulnerable Alex still was. And she realized from the increasing intensity of his kisses that there wasn't going to be much time left to talk. "Do you believe now that we can make a life together even though you're practicing medicine?''

"All those years I was absorbing the wrong message from my parents' relationship. It's not that a doctor can't have a good marriage, it's just that he has to work harder at it. I've begun limiting my practice,'' Alex said. "I realize now that I'm not cut out to be the workaholic my father was. I'm a good doctor, but I won't let that keep me from being a good husband or a good father.''

Jessica drew in her breath at his last words. "Do you want children?''

"One red-haired little girl, at least.''

"One brown-haired little boy, too,'' Jessica countered, putting her arms around Alex's neck and pulling him closer. "Just think, we'll be making Lydia a grandmother."

"If you don't stop looking at me with that seductive gleam in your eye, Jessie, we might start working on it before we can get the wedding license."

Jessica heard the question in his words and also the declaration of his willingness to wait for lovemaking until they were married. "Do you like long engagements?" she asked solemnly.

Alex shook his head. "Whatever the law demands is more my style," he said.

Jessica began to unbutton his shirt, her fingers absolutely steady. "You and I have so much in common," she said thoughtfully. "I'm surprised we didn't see it years ago."

"It's the things we don't have in common that are the most exciting," Alex answered. He waited until she was finished with his shirt before he sat up and flicked off a lamp near the sofa. Only the soft glow from the firelight illuminated the room.

Jessica admired the light sprinkling of golden hair covering his chest as he came back down to join her. She ran her hands over it, slipping his shirt off as she did to feel the rippling muscles of his back. "We're going to have a good life," she whispered, as he began to unbutton her blouse.

"*We* are," he agreed, his lips beginning to follow the path of his hands. "Beginning right now."

Jessica gave herself up to the feel of Alex's body against hers and to the loud angry blurt of his beeper. Beeper?

"Alex?" she said, pulling herself from her languor. "Why is your beeper beeping?"

Alex muttered something that sounded as if it was not meant for her ears and sat up. Self-consciously, Jessica pulled her blouse back together and sat up, too. "I've got to call my service," he said, running his hand through his hair.

Jessica wanted to pull the phone out of the wall, but she nodded instead. Alex was going to try to limit his practice; she would show him that she could be understanding about the normal demands of his job, even if she strangled on her own frustration. She watched him cross the room to the telephone and angrily punch a series of numbers. "Dr. Grainger," he grumbled into the receiver.

Alex listened for a moment, nodding his head. "Tell him to take two aspirins and call me in the morning," he said carelessly. He put the receiver back in its cradle, then seemed to think better of it. He lifted it again to drop it on the table. Then, with a flourish, he unhooked the beeper from his belt and threw it on the table beside the receiver. "Where were we?" he asked, his voice a spoken caress.

Jessica melted at the look in his eyes, but she couldn't let him off that easily. "You shouldn't have been so flippant," she admonished him. "What if that message was really serious?"

"The message was from my partner," he said, coming back to her side. "He was supposed to be on call for the evening, but he had something he had to take care of first. He just wanted our service to let me know that he's back on duty now."

"And we have the night together?"

Alex sat beside her and bent slowly to place his mouth on hers. "A small correction. We have the evening together. Lydia will never forgive me if I don't get you home by midnight."

"Then I'd suggest," Jessica said when she could talk again, "that you get down to the simple practice of medicine for the rest of our time together."

Alex raised an eyebrow. "Medicine?"

Jessica nodded slowly, slipping her blouse off her shoulders as he watched. "Yes. You see, I have a persistent ache that only you can cure."

Alex's eyes were alive with the glow of the firelight. "I think it may take a lifetime of treatment," he warned, his hands settling on her bare shoulders.

"Frequent treatment, I hope," Jessica said, meeting his gaze.

"Very, very frequent."

"Well, I'm not a doctor," she said, embracing him, "but it seems to me that the sooner we begin, the better my prognosis."

*   *   *   *   *

Silhouette

SPECIAL EDITION™

SPECIAL EDITION

Stories of love and life, these powerful
novels are tales that you can identify with—
romances with "something special" added
in!

Fall in love with the stories of authors such
as **Nora Roberts, Diana Palmer, Ginna Gray**
and many more of your special favorites—as
well as wonderful new voices!

Special Edition brings you
entertainment for the heart!

SSE-GEN

SILHOUETTE®

Desire®

Do you want...

Dangerously handsome heroes

Evocative, everlasting love stories

Sizzling and tantalizing sensuality

Incredibly sexy miniseries like **MAN OF THE MONTH**

Red-hot romance

Enticing entertainment that can't be beat!

You'll find all of this, and much *more* each and every month in **SILHOUETTE DESIRE.** Don't miss these unforgettable love stories by some of romance's hottest authors. Silhouette Desire—where your fantasies will always come true....

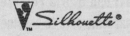

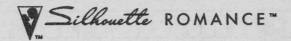

Silhouette ROMANCE™

What's a single dad to do when he needs a wife by next Thursday?

Who's a confirmed bachelor to call when he finds a baby on his doorstep?

How does a plain Jane in love with her gorgeous boss get him to notice her?

From classic love stories to romantic comedies to emotional heart tuggers, **Silhouette Romance** offers six irresistible novels every month by some of your favorite authors! Such as…beloved bestsellers **Diana Palmer, Annette Broadrick, Suzanne Carey, Elizabeth August** and **Marie Ferrarella,** to name just a few—and some sure to become favorites!

Fabulous Fathers…Bundles of Joy…Miniseries… Months of blushing brides and convenient weddings… Holiday celebrations… You'll find all this and much more in **Silhouette Romance**—always emotional, always enjoyable, always about love!